New Year's at the Graff

New Year's at the Graff

A Holiday at the Graff Romance

Marin Thomas

TULE
PUBLISHING

Chapter One

L ATE SUNDAY AFTERNOON Lucas Kendrick parked the
rental car in front of the Sunset Apartments on First
Avenue in Marietta, Montana. A handful of residents had
decorated for the holidays, but the strands of colored lights
strung over the doors failed to disguise the building's shabby
appearance. Despite the frigid temperature this last day of
December and six inches of snow on the ground, a pair of
bicycles, a skateboard and a kids' Big Wheel sat on the
sidewalk.

His gaze swung to unit 10—the downstairs apartment
his mother had lived in the first two years of Lucas's life. He
imagined a stroller parked on the stoop and a nineteen-year-
old single mom pushing her baby down the block to her
waitressing job at the diner thirty years ago.

His mother had never told him about her wish to one
day return to this town and thank the residents who'd helped
them when they'd been down on their luck. He'd only
discovered the fact after she'd passed away and he'd found a
collection of notes she'd written during their stay in Marietta. He wished she'd mentioned her desire to return to the
town before she'd died because he would have gladly paid for
the trip and accompanied her to Montana.

Only nine months had transpired between his mother's diagnosis and her final breath. It had always been just the two of them and losing her had knocked Lucas to his knees. After she'd been cremated, he'd boxed up her belongings and had stowed them in a storage unit. This past summer on the two-year anniversary of her passing, he'd found the courage to sort through the possessions and he'd discovered that his mother had written her thoughts on pieces of scrap paper, cards and store receipts. It was the message scribbled on a place mat from the Main Street Diner that had stuck in his head.

We have to leave, Lucas. This place and these people are becoming our family. If we don't go now, we never will. I miss my mother and I'm certain once my parents see you, they'll forgive. I promise we'll come back here when you're older and we'll thank our friends again for taking us in when we had nowhere to go.

Wanting to preserve the notes, Lucas had painstakingly typed each message on his laptop and then saved the file to a flash drive. Twenty-nine years had passed since his mother had left Marietta. Time would tell how many *friends* were still here. If he'd had his choice though, he would have waited until summer to make the trip.

A few too many glasses of spiked eggnog at the company Christmas party and a loose tongue had sent him to Montana in the dead of winter. If he hadn't let it slip that he was Roger Belfour's *illegitimate* son and not the new company employee, he'd be back in San Diego walking barefoot along the beach. Unfortunately Claire had freaked out, accusing

Lucas of intentionally humiliating her in front of her high-society friends and she'd banned him from celebrating the holidays with the family.

In an effort to keep the peace, Roger had asked Lucas to take an extended vacation. Frustrated and a little hurt that his father had bowed to his wife's demands, Lucas had chosen to serve out his banishment in the treasure state. Thanking a handful of people on his mother's behalf would be a nice diversion from the hostile Belfour family.

Growing up Lucas had always wished for a father, but once he'd turned eighteen and learned who'd sired him, he had no desire to establish a relationship with the man, believing his mother deserved his loyalty because she'd made all the sacrifices and had raised Lucas alone.

Several Google searches had turned up a windfall of information on Roger Belfour, the CEO of Belfour Property Investments in San Diego. He had a wife and two sons a few years older than Lucas, which meant Roger, had cheated on Claire with Lucas's mom. Lucas had asked about the affair, but his mother had dodged the questions, and he'd always wondered what she was hiding.

Life went on and Lucas had enrolled in college and focused on earning a business degree. After graduation he went to work as a business analyst for a grocery-store chain. He might never have reached out to Roger if his mother hadn't asked him to before she'd died.

When Lucas met Roger in person for the first time he'd been surprised by their physical resemblance—Lucas looked more like his father than his half brothers did. What was supposed to have been a brief meeting had turned into a job offer and before Lucas had stopped to consider the ramifications, he'd accepted a position in Roger Belfour's company.

He found out quickly that although his father was happy to have him working at the office, Claire, Seth and Brady objected to Lucas's presence. Claire had warned Lucas that she'd be keeping a close eye on him and his half brothers accused Lucas on a daily basis of trying to make them look bad—which wasn't hard to do when the men took three-hour lunches and spent most of the day reading online dating profiles.

Because Roger took a firm stand against firing his *illegitimate son*, Lucas was motivated to work hard on behalf of Belfour Investments. He was sure that once he proved he had the company's best interests at heart, Claire and his half brothers would accept him and he'd be part of a family—something he'd always wished for growing up.

He glanced at the dashboard clock—he'd been parked in front of the apartments for fifteen minutes. He better leave before one of the tenants called the police and reported a suspicious man lurking in their neighborhood. Lucas drove off, keeping his eyes peeled for the Graff Hotel. The rental car didn't have a GPS system but the town's population was only a little over ten thousand—it shouldn't be difficult to find an old hotel.

He'd driven a block when he noticed a middle-aged woman with bright orange hair, brushing the snow off of a menagerie of plaster of paris wildlife in her yard. Her tiny turquoise home was an eyesore. Instead of the traditional evergreen, a fuchsia wreath hung on the front door. Snow-flake decals covered the house windows and three-foot-tall candy canes lined both sides of the walk. Plastic replicas of Santa, the Abominable Snowman and the Island of Misfit Toys stood near a sleigh pulled by four prancing reindeer—one with a missing leg.

Green extension cords crisscrossed the snow, supplying power to the lights wrapped around an oak tree with a smirking Grinch leaning against the trunk. Lucas smiled, thinking his mother would have loved the gaudy holiday display.

He lowered the passenger-side window. "Excuse me, ma'am."

The Lucille Ball look-alike approached the car, her curls bouncing around her head. She rested the broom against the door and then stuck her head through the window. Her gaze zigzagged between Lucas and the empty passenger seat. "Good afternoon," she said.

"I'm looking for the Graff Hotel."

She pointed west. "Two blocks that way across the rail-road tracks."

"Thank you."

"Are you here for the ball?"

"What ball?" he asked.

"The Big Sky Mavericks Ball at the Graff." She smiled. "The charitable group is raising money to update the fair-grounds and rebuild the grandstand."

"I don't know anything about a party for the fair-grounds." When he'd booked his room he hadn't been told there'd be a New Year's Eve bash at the hotel.

Her eyes shifted to the empty passenger seat again. "You didn't hear?"

There was something peculiar about the woman. "Hear what?"

She looked at him. "The fairgrounds caught fire last year and they had to cancel the annual Copper Mountain Rodeo. Thank goodness, no one was injured." Tiny white puffs of air escaped her mouth as she continued to talk. "The sheriff's department suspects arson, but they're still investigating."

Despite her nose and ears turning pink from the frigid temps, the woman would continue talking if Lucas didn't end the conversation. "Thank you for the directions." His finger hovered over the button to raise the window, but her gloved hand remained on the doorframe.

"You should go to the ball," she said.

He was better off avoiding parties after the ruckus he'd caused at the last one he'd attended. "I don't have a tux."

The red curls shook. "It's a rodeo-themed party. Boots, western shirts and—" she winked at the seat next to him "—big belt buckles."

Yep, the lady was an oddball.

She grabbed the broom and backed away from the car.

"I didn't get your name," he said.

"Tilly."

The name sounded like a cartoon character's moniker.

"Have fun at the ball, Lucas." She went into her house, leaving the broom on the porch.

Not until he'd pulled into the parking lot of the Graff

Hotel, did Lucas realize that the redhead had called him by name. He couldn't remember if he'd introduced himself or not. A bellman appeared as soon as he stepped from the rental car.

"Good afternoon, sir. May I help with your bags?"

"Thanks, I appreciate it." Lucas pressed the key fob to unlock the trunk then took his briefcase and followed the bellman into the hotel where he came face-to-face with a giant fur tree covered in glass ornaments, tiny white lights and wide velvet ribbons. He had to crane his neck to see the star at the top—an inch below the lobby's vaulted ceiling.

"Welcome to the Graff, sir."

Lucas glanced at the bellman's nametag. "Thank you, Ron." He nodded to the tables displaying a variety of gingerbread houses. "What's all this?"

"Marietta's annual gingerbread-house competition." Ron walked over to a house with a blue ribbon attached to its copper-colored cookie roof. "Copper Mountain Chic won the award this year in the merchant's category."

Ron set the luggage by the check-in desk and tapped the silver bell on the counter. "The ski slopes will be crowded after the dusting of snow heading our way in a couple of days."

"I don't ski." Lucas preferred warm sand between his toes not icy snow.

"They offer free lessons on the bunny slope. If you change your mind, the Graff rents ski equipment." Ron backed up a step when a young man wearing navy pants, a white dress shirt and a navy blazer appeared behind the desk.

Lucas reached into his jean pocket for the five-dollar bill he'd gotten in change after buying coffee at the airport. He handed the money to the bellman. "Appreciate your help."

"Thank you, sir. Enjoy your stay."

"Welcome to the Graff, Mr.—"

"Kendrick. Lucas Kendrick." He set his credit card on the counter.

"I'm Bob." The employee smiled. "It will take just a moment to check you in."

When Lucas agreed to vanish for a while, his father had insisted he use the company credit card to pay for his hotel and meals. He was only too happy to spend Roger's money, figuring once Claire saw the bill for his mini-vacation she'd think twice about exiling him when he accidently offended her.

"Mr. Kendrick," Bob said, "I'll need the license plate number of the car you're driving."

Lucas took the rental agreement out of his briefcase.

"Thank you."

While Bob finished checking him in, he studied the lobby's opulence, wondering if his mother had ever stepped foot inside the hotel.

Despite the holiday décor there was no disguising the elegance of the historic building. Marble floors, tall columns and rich walnut paneling catered to the privileged and wealthy.

"You'll be staying on the third floor, Mr. Kendrick." Bob held out a keycard. "Room 311." He motioned to his right. "The bank of elevators is around the corner and—" his finger swung in the other direction "—the stairs are on the other side of the tree." The desk attendant held up a glossy notecard with the words *Boots, Chaps & Cowboy Hats* printed across the front. "We're offering hotel guests a discount on tickets for tonight's New Year's Eve party."

"I'll pass, thank you."

"It's for a great cause, sir and—" Bob's gaze traveled over Lucas "—if I may say so, you look like a man who gambles."

Lucas had never considered himself a gambler but he'd taken a huge one when he'd reached out to his biological father, and Roger hadn't slammed the door in his face.

Bob continued his sales pitch but Lucas stopped listening when he heard feminine laughter behind him. He turned and spotted a petite brunette in a hotel uniform speaking with Ron. The bellman helped her on with her coat and when she turned to put her arms through the sleeves, her gaze clashed with Lucas's. As if the marble floor had turned to quicksand, Lucas felt himself being sucked into deep, dark pools of luminous brown. Then a cold blast of air swept through the lobby, breaking the spell. The woman's lashes fluttered down and she looked away.

"Sir?"

A deep voice cut through Lucas's fogged brain and he turned to the desk clerk. "I'm sorry. What were you saying?"

"The party will be held in the main ballroom and there'll be lots of casino-style games. Appetizers will be served until midnight and a cash bar will be open until one a.m."

More cold air hit the back of his legs and he glanced over his shoulder and watched the brown-eyed beauty leave the hotel. He tracked her progress across the parking lot to a small compact vehicle. After she opened the door and tossed her purse inside, she looked back at the building. She couldn't see into the lobby because of the tinted windows but maybe she'd felt the same zap of excitement as he had when they'd stared into each other's eyes.

"Would you like to attend the ball, sir?"

Lucas tapped his knuckles against the counter. "Hold that thought, Bob." He walked over to the bellman. "Ron."

"May I help you, sir?"

How did he tell the bellman that it was imperative he meet the woman who'd just left the hotel without sounding like a stalker? "The lady…"

"Which lady would that be, sir?"

Why did the woman feel familiar? "She was wearing a hotel uniform."

"Yes, sir."

Ron didn't offer a name—he was protecting the employee's identity. Lucas stared out the window, catching the back end of her car as it left the lot. He'd dated his share of women and had one semi-serious relationship but he'd never felt this desperate urgency to know more about a woman he'd never met before. "Forget it, Ron."

"Sir." The bellman's eyes glinted with humor. "She'll be back later to help out with the casino games in the ballroom."

Lucas smiled his thanks then returned to the desk. "Bob, it looks like I'll be going to the ball after all."

"The ticket is forty dollars, Mr. Kendrick."

Lucas removed the cash from his wallet and Bob handed him the invitation. "You won't regret going, sir."

Especially if Lucas ran into the brown-eyed goddess.

"Would you like Ron to take your things to your room while you relax in the bar?"

"No, thank you."

"If there's anything the staff can do to make your stay more enjoyable please don't hesitate to ask."

Lucas wheeled his suitcase to the bank of elevators and rode to the third floor. When the doors opened, plush carpet, gilded lighting and more walnut woodwork greeted him. He keyed into the room, turned on the lights and then stepped back in time to the early 1900s. The queen-size bed sported a fancy wrought-iron headboard and the navy duvet matched the floor-length curtains on the window overlooking the railroad tracks behind the hotel. An antique slant-front mahogany desk sat in one corner and a mini fridge had been tucked beneath the table near a leather chair and ottoman.

He poked his head inside the en-suite bathroom. The black-and-white penny tile and claw-foot tub were a nice touch. Light gray towels and an array of high-end bath products sat on the marble countertop. Even the toilet tissue was fancy—the end piece folded into a fan.

He returned to the bedroom, hung up his coat and opened the complimentary bottle of water on the TV stand then picked up the chocolate treat that had been left on the bed pillow. He rubbed his thumb over the foil wrapper, wondering if the brown-eyed angel had placed the chocolate on his pillow.

Lucas shook his head. How could a stranger completely mesmerize him?

Before he got carried away with his fantasy, he kicked off his shoes and then connected his laptop to the Internet so he could check email. Unbeknownst to his father or half brothers, Lucas had reached out to his alumni contacts at the W.P. Carey School of Business at Arizona State University and had struck up a conversation with Stan Mueller. Mueller was a well-known developer who turned unique properties into loft apartments and high-end condos for the wealthy.

Stan's work had been highlighted in major magazines and his properties could be found in New York City, Miami and Los Angeles as well as smaller cities like Aspen, Colorado, and Jackson Hole, Wyoming. Stan said he'd entertain doing a business deal with Belfour Investments if Lucas found a unique property. Lucas was flying under the radar on this project because he didn't want his father to get his hopes up. But a deal with Mueller would take Roger's company to the next level and show Claire and his half brothers that Lucas wasn't out to sabotage his father's business.

"THE PRINCE AND Cinderella lived happily ever after in the prince's castle."

Ava Moore closed the picture book then removed Sophie's eyeglasses and set them on the nightstand. "Be good for Nana while I'm working tonight." She kissed her daughter's forehead and smoothed the curls away from her face.

"Is Cinderella gonna be at the ball?" Her daughter's stare fixated on Ava, reminding her of the man she'd seen checking in to the hotel after her shift had ended a few hours ago. An entire lobby had separated them, but it had felt like he'd been standing right in front of her.

"No, honey. There won't be any Cinderellas or princes." The town of Marietta was fresh out of princes—at least any who were interested in a widow with a four-year-old child. *Don't forget Tilly.*

At least any princes who were interested in a widow with a four-year-old child and an eccentric mother-in-law.

Ava preferred using the word *eccentric*—it was kinder than the name the neighborhood kids used—silly Tilly.

"Was my daddy a prince?" Sophie asked.

"He was a handsome prince." Especially when Drew had dressed in his air force uniform.

"Princes aren't supposed to die," Sophie said.

"Sometimes accidents happen and princes get hurt." Two years ago Drew had been crushed by a piece of equipment while helping to move a missile at the Malmstrom Air Force Base. He'd died only a month after they'd transferred to Great Falls, Montana, where he'd been assigned to the 341st Missile Wing.

"Nana said Daddy was a rebel. What's a rebel?"

"A rebel is someone who is brave and fearless."

And reckless. And rude. And loud. Boisterous. Egotistical.

Ava hadn't been able to resist Drew's bad-boy ways when

he'd strolled into the restaurant in Louisiana where she'd been a waitress and had announced that he was the guy she'd been waiting for all of her life. His bold personality had appealed to a twenty-two-year-old girl still living with the elderly foster parents who'd taken her in at the age of thirteen.

She'd thought Drew would settle down after they'd married but he'd preferred to hang out with his air force buddies and act single. When she'd become pregnant she'd hoped fatherhood would tame his wild ways but that hadn't happened, either. After she'd voiced her concern that he wasn't spending enough time with her and Sophie, Drew had become defensive, insisting that parenting was her role and protecting the country was his.

"I want to go to the ball," Sophie whined.

"Children aren't allowed to gamble." Instead of turning down beds at the hotel tonight, Ava and the rest of the housekeeping staff were running the casino-style gaming tables.

"How come Nana isn't going?"

"Because she's watching you." Her mother-in-law had offered to sleep at the apartment tonight, so Ava wouldn't have to wake Sophie to take her home when she returned after midnight.

Tilly was only fifty-two but her mind wandered and she'd been involved in a handful of minor car accidents and cited for inattentive driving. Tilly never drove Sophie anywhere but last month her mother-in-law had gone to the diner for supper and instead of putting the car into park, she'd left it in neutral. A waitress had spotted the driverless vehicle moving down Main Street and luckily a customer was able to stop the car before it jumped the curb and plowed into the toy store. Unluckily for Tilly the police had asked her to surrender her license and now Ava held the keys to her mother-in-law's Buick.

A voice echoed from the other room—Tilly was talking to herself again. When Ava had moved to Marietta after Drew died, she'd been concerned by Tilly's one-sided conversations and had asked to accompany her mother-in-law to her yearly checkup with the doctor she'd been seeing for over a decade. The physician had assured Ava there was nothing physically wrong with Tilly and that several years ago she'd undergone a battery of psychological tests, which were inconclusive. In other words, Ava's mother-in-law marched to her own drum.

"I have to leave, honey." She gave her daughter one more kiss.

"Night, Mommy."

Ava pulled the covers up to Sophie's chin then turned off the lights and left the room. Tilly sat on the couch, knitting a cuddle cocoon. Her mother-in-law had been making the baby pouches for years and donated them to the Marietta Regional Hospital. Each baby born in the hospital left in a blue or pink cocoon. Tilly's cocoons were cherished keep-sakes and the new mothers raved over the tiny baby sea turtles she knitted around the opening of the sacks.

"I like your sparkly shirt," Tilly said.

"Thank you." Ava shrugged into her coat. Hotel employees were required to dress as cowgirls or cowboys for the party. Fortunately she owned several pairs of jeans and a pair of black cowgirl boots. She'd picked up the pink rhinestone shirt at a second-hand store in Livingston. "If it gets too chilly in here feel free to turn up the heat."

"We'll be fine."

"I'll lock up." Ava stepped outside, closed the door and then used the apartment key to turn the dead bolt. Carefully, she descended the fire-escape stairs, clutching the cold handrail. Once her feet reached the pavement, she hurried to her Toyota parked by the Dumpster. A blast of cold wind whipped her long ponytail into the air as she ducked inside the car.

While she waited for the engine to warm, her thoughts turned to the future. She was looking forward to the Tuesday morning meeting with her landlord, Sandra Reynolds. Sandra owned the building and Copper Mountain Chic, the upscale clothing boutique on the first floor below Ava's apartment. She didn't want to get ahead of herself, but she hoped to talk Sandra into partnering with her co-op to help single mothers further their education.

Ava turned at the courthouse then drove one block to Front Avenue and parked on the street across from the Graff. At 7:45 p.m. the lot was crowded with vehicles. Casino night kicked off at eight o'clock but the party was already in full swing. She wondered if she'd run into the handsome man she locked gazes with earlier in the lobby. Ava hadn't dated since Drew had passed away—she'd been busy finishing her business degree and developing plans for the co-op. And it had been a long time since a man had made her feel desirable.

Whoa, girl. Ava was getting ahead of herself. Just because she'd felt a connection to the stranger didn't mean anything had to come of it. He'd been checking in to the hotel, which meant he wasn't local and she wasn't falling for a man who'd eventually leave town. She'd followed Drew from Louisiana to Montana and look at how disastrous the outcome had been. The last thing she wanted to do was move her and her daughter for another man and then end up alone again.

When she entered the lobby, Bob waved her over to the front desk.

"Angelica left a cowboy hat for you in the employee coatroom," he said.

"Yee-haw." Ava stowed her jacket and gloves, then flung her ponytail over her shoulder and put on the hat. Pasting a smile on her face she headed for the makeshift casino, keeping a lookout for those mysterious blue eyes.

Chapter Two

F OR THE PAST ten minutes Lucas had been standing near the ballroom doors in the Graff Hotel, searching the crowd of cowboys and cowgirls for the petite dark-haired woman he'd seen in the lobby a few hours ago. He slid his hand into his jean pocket and toyed with the flash drive he'd carried with him from California. He wondered if any of the older people milling about had known his mother or were on her list of people to thank.

"Not a gambler?" An elderly gentleman dressed more like a cattle baron than a cowboy stopped in front of Lucas.

"No, sir. You?"

"I'd rather write a check to a charity than suffer through this nonsense." He held out his hand. "Alistair Kingsley."

"Lucas Kendrick."

The old man sipped his drink. "My wife dragged me to this party. According to her I need to work on my social skills."

"I hear the money raised tonight will help update the fairgrounds."

"I'd rather see Marietta focus on attracting young professionals to this town than spend its money on a once-a-year event like the rodeo."

Lucas's ears perked. "What's stopping younger business people from settling in Marietta?"

"Housing is limited to single-family homes and a couple of apartment complexes. We need high-end condos and townhomes."

"The stores looked busy this afternoon when I drove down Main Street," Lucas said.

"There are several successful businesses in Marietta but we could use more." The old man shoved his hand into his trouser pocket. "Things turned around for Marietta when Troy Sheenan bought the Graff in 2010 and saved it from demolition."

"What happened to the hotel before Sheenan purchased it?"

"Bankruptcy. They boarded up the windows and barred the doors in 1982."

Lucas had been born in 1987. That meant his mother had never seen the inside of the hotel when they'd lived in Marietta.

Kingsley pointed to the wood-paneled door Lucas had propped his shoulder against. "Sheenan didn't cut any corners when he restored the building. After it opened again in 2013, tourism picked up but it wasn't until the Graff celebrated its 100-year anniversary in 2014 that the town experienced a consistent uptick in tourism."

"By tourism you mean outdoor enthusiasts."

"Our close proximity to Copper Mountain makes it an ideal getaway for winter skiing. In the summer Miracle Lake and the Marietta River draw fishermen and kayakers. The young kids like tubing down the river."

"I bet there are plenty of hiking trails and rock climbing areas," Lucas said.

"We've got everything from cross-country skiing to snow shoeing to B&Bs and dude ranches."

"If you don't mind me asking," Lucas said, "what do you do for a living?"

"I'm a family court judge. Semi-retired. I'll be eighty-six soon and I'm trying to convince my wife to get rid of her business so we can travel before I end up in a sanatorium."

"Where is your wife's business located?"

"Main Street. In the heart of downtown Marietta. The building was once a mercantile and apothecary shop in the early 1900s. After Sandra purchased it, she restored the original interior."

The more Lucas learned about the building the more intrigued he grew. "What kind of restoration work did she have done?"

"Exposing the brick walls and copper piping. She paid a fortune to restore the original wood floors."

This was exactly the kind of property Stan Mueller developed into upscale apartments for young professionals. Lucas grinned. "Maybe I can help support your cause."

"How's that, young man?"

"I work for Belfour Investments in San Diego. I know a developer who buys vintage properties and turns them into expensive condos and apartments."

The judge waved his hand in the air and a regal-looking woman with a sleek silver bob walked over. She slid her arm through the judge's and gazed at him as if he were a young Clark Gable and not a man on the wrong side of eighty. "What do you need, dear?"

"This is Lucas Kendrick, a businessman from San Diego. Lucas, my wife, Sandra Reynolds." The judge cleared his throat. "Lucas knows a developer who might be interested in your building. You could let him have a look at Copper Mountain Chic."

"Copper Mountain Chic?" Lucas pointed over his shoulder toward the lobby. "You won an award in the gingerbread competition this year."

Sandra smiled.

"I was telling Lucas that I'd like to travel with my wife before I die."

She rolled her eyes. "He's so dramatic for a judge, isn't he?" She rose on tiptoes and kissed his wrinkled cheek. "If you're willing to take me on a trip around the world, then I'll consider selling."

"Done," the judge said. "Tell Lucas when you're available to talk business."

She laughed. "Stop by Copper Mountain Chic the day after tomorrow and we'll chat." She tugged on her husband's arm. "Let's dance."

"Are you trying to give me a heart attack before I've booked our plane tickets?"

Sandra smiled at Lucas. "The shop opens at ten."

"I'll be there." It was a stroke of luck meeting the judge tonight. Maybe Lucas would test his good fortune in the casino. He walked further into the room, passing by the card

MARIN THOMAS

tables, then put the brakes on when he spotted the attractive brown-eyed cowgirl manning the dice table.

This was his lucky night after all.

⟫⟫⟪⟪

AVA BENT DOWN to pick up the pen she'd dropped on the floor and felt a chilly burst of air rush past her. Maybe the hotel manager had switched on the air conditioning because the room was growing crowded. She glanced up at the ceiling but there was no vent above the table. That was odd. When she stood up again she came face-to-face with the handsome man who'd captured her interest earlier in the day.

Oh. My. Goodness. He was even better looking up close.

A fluttering sensation erupted in her stomach gaining in strength with each pounding beat of her heart.

"Good evening." He smiled.

She returned his smile.

"Lucas Kendrick." He held out his hand.

"Ava Moore." When his fingers wrapped around hers, the nerves along the surface of her skin vibrated with electricity.

"Ava's a beautiful name." He was staring again—just like he'd done in the lobby. A gaze so intense she felt as if his eyes could see inside her body.

"Are you enjoying your stay at the hotel, Mr. Kendrick?"

"Lucas. Please."

"Lucas," she said because she wanted to find out how his name felt on her tongue. Verdict—smooth, subtle, addicting.

He was several inches taller than Ava's five-foot-six height and when he moved closer to the table she had to crane her neck to look him in the eye. And what beautiful eyes... His electric-blue gaze mesmerized her. When his stare drifted to her mouth, her insides lifted up as if she was floating on air and she curled her fingers into the palms of her hands to anchor herself.

"I just arrived in town today from California, but so far I'm enjoying my stay at the Graff."

"It's definitely our main attraction." She showed him a plastic cup. "Would you like to roll the dice and take your chances?"

"I think I would."

"The object is to beat the dealer. I roll first. If you end up with a higher number, you win."

"And the prize?" His voice was as deep and inviting as his blue eyes.

She pointed to the bin filled with Copper Mountain Rodeo koozies. "If you lose, you pay the house a dollar for each of our combined points."

He slid onto a stool in front of the table. "I can't very well leave town without a souvenir koozie."

She dropped the pair of dice into the cup, shook it, and then dumped them onto the felt cloth. "Seven." She left her dice on the table and dropped a second pair into the cup before handing it to Lucas. "Good luck."

A pair of fours spilled onto the table. He beat the house by one point. She handed him a koozie. "Congratulations,

Lucas."

He set the prize aside. "It never hurts to have an extra koozie on hand."

"Ah, a two-fisted drinker?" She struggled to keep a straight face and threw the dice. "Four. That shouldn't be difficult to beat."

He rolled a three and she laughed. "You owe the house seven dollars." She placed a pad of paper on the table. "Would you like to keep a tab?"

His blue eyes twinkled. "I believe I would."

Ava threw a six.

"You work at the hotel." He threw a five.

She added eleven dollars to the total. "Housekeeping." She threw an eight.

He tossed a nine and she handed him a second koozie. "Are you in town on business or pleasure?" She winced the moment the question had escaped her mouth. Small talk was part of her job tonight, but she hadn't meant to insinuate that she was interested in more than a game of dice with him.

"A little of both," he said.

When he didn't elaborate, she shook the cup and threw the dice. "Nine."

"Eight," he said.

She added seventeen dollars to his tab. "Would you like to set a limit?"

He shook his head. "You have a slight Southern accent, but I can't place it."

"Northwest Louisiana. I grew up in Bossier City."

"How did a Louisiana girl end up in Montana?"

"She married an airman who was transferred to Malmstrom Air Force Base in Great Falls."

His gaze dropped to Ava's bare ring finger then returned to her face.

"He died." She cringed at the confession. This was a New Year's Eve party. The last thing she should be discussing with a guest was her deceased husband.

"I'm sorry." He held her gaze, the intense color of his eyes fading to the soft blue of a mid-winter sky. "It's not easy losing someone you love."

And it was no easier losing someone you'd already fallen out of love with. "Thank you."

"I don't know what it feels like to lose a spouse, but I was very close to my mother," he said, "and she passed away two years ago."

"I'm so sorry."

"How long has your husband been gone?"

"The same. Two years." Ava had attended grief counseling before packing her and Sophie's belongings and moving to Marietta. Once she'd left the base, she'd promised herself she would focus on the future and not look back. She shook the cup and the dice spilled onto the table. "Five."

Lucas threw a nine and she handed him another prize. "Maybe you'd like to try a different game before you end up with a suitcase full of koozies."

The twinkle was back in his eyes. "I like the company at this table."

Her cheeks warmed and she tossed the dice again. "Six."

He threw a five and she added an eleven to his tab. "You're at forty-six dollars." When he didn't object, she threw the dice again. "Pair of sixes."

Lucas came up with three. Fifteen dollars went on the tab. After a few more turns she added thirty dollars to the total. "Ninety-one."

"Keep going."

She rolled an eight and he rolled a six. "That's one hundred and five dollars," she said.

"When do you get off work tonight?" He looked away for a moment then made eye contact with her and said, "I'm sorry. That was a little bold."

Ava was flattered that he was interested in her, but her life was crazy busy and this man was just passing through town. "I'm working until one a.m. then I turn into a pumpkin."

He chuckled. "I don't think you could look like a pumpkin even on your worst day." He pointed to the disco ball dangling in the center of the room. "You'll be here when the clock strikes midnight?"

The air in her lungs escaped in a soft whoosh, carrying the word "yes" across the table.

"I believe I'll pay my tab then try the card games."

"Lucas." This time when his gaze connected with hers, there were flecks of silver in the blue orbs. "Big Sky Mavericks thanks you for your support."

After he disappeared into the crowd, Ava's boss Angelica Puente stopped by the table. "How did it go?"

"Mr. Kendrick donated a hundred and five dollars to the

fundraiser."

"I wasn't asking how much money he lost." Angelica lowered her voice. "What do you think of him?"

"He's nice. Why?"

"Did you find out his age?"

"It's hotel policy not to ask guests personal questions."

"He's a perfect match for you."

Ava's gaze darted across the room. Lucas sat at the blackjack table conversing with Judge Kingsley. She couldn't help comparing Lucas to her deceased husband. Drew would never have given an old man like the judge the time of day. "He lives in California."

"California is a hop, skip and a jump away from Montana."

Ava rolled her eyes. "He'll be gone in a day or two."

"Maybe not." Angelica lowered her voice. "His hotel reservation is open-ended."

"How do you know that?"

"I overheard Bob talking with Ron in the lobby earlier today."

If people thought secrets were difficult to keep in small towns, they should work at a hotel in a small town.

"And Ron said Mr. Kendrick asked him who you were—" Angelica held up a hand. "Don't worry, Ron didn't tell him your name or where you live. But when Ron said that you were working at the ball tonight, Mr. Kendrick changed his mind and bought a ticket to the event."

Ava felt like a giddy schoolgirl after learning Lucas had come to the ball to meet her.

Angelica touched Ava's arm. "I'm just giving you a nudge, because I care about you."

Ava had been employed at the hotel longer than Angelica but she'd quickly bonded with her boss when she'd discovered how much they had in common despite their age difference. They'd spent part of their childhood in foster care, were single mothers and had daughters whose fathers had died. Angelica was like an older sister whom Ava looked to for advice and support. "Maybe *you* should ask Lucas out. You haven't dated since you moved to Marietta."

"Lucas isn't interested in a forty-three-year-old."

"He's from California. He might like cougars."

Angelica laughed. "Any man who wants to date me has to get past my grandfather-in-law and no one will ever be good enough to replace Judge Kingsley's grandson." Angelica checked the clock on the wall. "I need to make sure Ron's ready to dim the lights."

It was ten minutes before midnight and Ava doubted any gamblers would stop by the dice table for one last roll. She grabbed a hand broom and a dustpan and swept up the floor—popcorn kernels, bits of paper and a shriveled-up olive from someone's martini.

She dumped the debris in a trash can then returned to her station. When she bent down to put the broom away, she spotted a flash drive under the table. Big Sky Mavericks had ordered dozens of drives imprinted with their name to use as prizes at several of the tables but this one was missing the logo.

"One minute until midnight!" a voice shouted.

She didn't have time to toss the drive into the trash across the room, so she dropped it into her pocket and hurried to put away the items at her table.

"Thirty seconds!"

She folded the felt cloth and shoved it into a plastic bag then tossed in the cup, dice and remaining koozies. She glanced at the crowd gathering beneath the disco ball, but didn't spot Lucas. Maybe he'd changed his mind and had left the party. Scolding herself for being disappointed, she turned to leave and found Lucas blocking her path.

He grasped her shoulders, his stare hypnotizing her.

"Ten!"

His hands trailed down her arms then his fingers slid between hers and held them tight.

Her reflection danced in his eyes, and she was shocked at the yearning she saw.

"Nine…eight…"

His gaze slid to her mouth, his chest rising and falling in rhythm with Ava's breaths.

"Seven…"

Only a sliver of blue was visible around his dilated pupils.

"Six…five…"

The scent of his cologne enveloped her in a warm hug and she swayed forward, clasping his forearms to steady herself.

"Four…three…two…"

His face drew closer, his breath sliding over her chin, rolling across her heated flesh. Then he held her face between his hands as if he cradled a precious object.

"Happy New Year!"

Ava's lashes drifted closed when his mouth brushed across her lips.

The room exploded with sound—party horns, popping balloons and noisemakers—but Ava only heard the soft melody of Lucas's kiss. The lights came on and he moved his head so that his lips brushed against her ear when he whispered, "Happy New Year, Ava." A burst of cold air drifted down the back of her shirt when he walked away and she shivered as confetti rained down on her.

"He kissed you."

Ava snapped out of her trance and looked at her boss. "Did anyone else see?"

Angelica nodded across the room. Ron grinned and waved. *Great.* The next time she showed up for her housekeeping shift all of her co-workers would know what happened tonight.

"Is he a decent kisser?"

Ava felt her cheeks grow warm. Lucas's kiss had been more than decent—it had been sexy. Hot. And he'd breathed her in when his lips had caressed hers.

"I think you should ask him out."

Ava opened her mouth to object but Angelica held up a hand.

"I know he doesn't live in Marietta and you're a single mom with a young daughter, but there's no reason you can't get to know him better. Find out what he does for a living. Maybe he's a salesman and he'll be visiting Marietta often."

Ava frowned. She wasn't interested in a casual relationship.

"The room's emptying out," Angelica said. "Will you collect the tablecloths?"

Ava grabbed the white coverings then followed her boss to the laundry facility where Angelica loaded the linens into three industrial-size washers. Ava sat at the folding table and Angelica joined her.

"I'm probably the last person who should be giving advice but I'm speaking from experience when I say that life goes by fast."

Ava was only twenty-six but the life she'd lived so far made her feel a lot older. "I get the whole live-in-the-moment thing but I have Sophie's feelings to think about. She doesn't even remember her dad. If another man comes into her life and then disappears shortly afterward, she'll get her heart broken."

"I was insinuating that women have needs just like men and—"

"I should have a fling?" Ava crossed her arms over her chest.

Angelica stared at Ava like a bug under a microscope. "I wasn't going to say fling. I was going to say that after you get to know him better you might discover that what you feel for him goes deeper than sexual attraction."

How could Ava explain that after a few heated looks and a single kiss her feelings for Lucas had already moved beyond a one-night stand? "It's the eyes."

"What about his eyes?"

"When he stares at me I can't look away. It's just the two us. Standing in front of each other." *Wanting each other.*

"If we're always focused on looking down the road, we'll never take time to stop and smell the proverbial roses."

Ava conceded that she was guilty of working too hard. Of being responsible with her money. Of making good choices. Abiding by the rules. "I'll give it some thought," she said. "Right now I need to go home and sleep. I have to be back here tomorrow at ten."

Angelica squeezed Ava's hand. "I hate seeing you alone."

Ava hugged her supervisor then returned to the employee lounge, put on her coat and gloves and walked into the lobby. "Happy New Year, Ron."

He opened the door and smiled. "The year is starting off with a bang, isn't it?"

The only bang Ava wanted to hear was the cork popping on a champagne bottle when her co-op opened to the public.

Chapter Three

Ava pushed the housekeeping cart down the hall, stopping in front of room 311. A few doors over an older couple stepped out of their room and hung the Do Not Disturb sign on the door handle.

One less room to clean. "Enjoy your day." She smiled at the pair when they passed her on the way to the elevator.

She keyed into 311 and flipped on the lights. A quick glance around told her that only one person occupied the room—a considerate person. Ava had cleaned rooms where the guests had used the trash can as a basketball hoop and the floor had been littered with wrappers and empty water bottles. Once she'd even found a sopping wet bath towel left on one of the beds.

Ava peeked into the bathroom. The guest had left the dirty towels in the tub. The soap dish wasn't sitting in a puddle of water on the counter and there was no toothpaste spit on the mirror, which meant the guest kept their head down while they brushed their teeth instead of fixating on their face. Ava believed that the more toothpaste splatter on a mirror the more conceited the person.

When she reached into the tub to scoop up the towels, a woodsy scent drifted up her nose. Last night after the ball when she'd returned to her apartment and had crawled into bed, she swore she smelled Lucas's cologne—hints of lavender, coumarin and oak moss—the same scent she'd caught a whiff of moments ago.

Ava deposited the towels in the dirty linen bag on the cart in the hallway then grabbed a fresh set of towels and the disinfectant spray before returning to the bathroom. Ten minutes later the room gleamed and she folded the end of the toilet paper into a fan before closing the door behind her. Next, she opened the curtains and sunlight flooded the room.

The guest had left a *Green* housekeeping card on the bed, electing not to have their sheets changed today. She placed the card back on the TV stand then returned to the cart for a piece of chocolate to put on the pillow.

"How are things on the floor?" Angelica asked when she stepped off the elevator.

"It's a light day." Ava nodded down the hall. "I counted four Do Not Disturb signs." She pointed to the cleaning chart hanging from the side of the cart. "Three more rooms after this one then I'm finished."

Angelica's gaze swung to the open doorway behind Ava. "Have you found out anything interesting about him?"

"I'm not following?"

"Room 311."

"What about it?" Ava asked.

Angelica leaned closer. "Lucas Kendrick is staying in that room." She smiled and walked off.

Ava returned to the room then stood by the unmade bed,

staring at the rumpled sheets. No wonder the bath towels had smelled familiar—it was Lucas's cologne. She took his pillow and turned to place it on the leather chair but instead she pressed it against her face and inhaled the heady scent of laundry detergent, cologne and Lucas. She closed her eyes and imagined him sprawled across the mattress, sleeping. A cold draft swept past her legs and a moment later a knock startled her.

"Ava."

She swallowed a gasp and dropped the pillow on the bed then spun around.

Lucas's lips spread into a wide smile.

She opened her mouth to say something—anything—but only the breath she'd been holding rushed past her lips.

"Hello, Ava." His voice sounded even deeper than she remembered. "I was about to make your bed then I'll be out of your way."

"You could never be in my way." He walked to the opposite side and said, "I'll help you."

Without breaking eye contact they reached for the end of the sheet and straightened it then repeated the process with the duvet before he watched her plump his pillow.

"Ava?"

"What?"

"This is crazy, but I swear it feels like I know you and I don't understand why."

She drew in a steadying breath but it made her feel light-headed.

"Have you ever been to San Diego?" he asked.

"No." She placed the piece of chocolate on his pillow.

His blue eyes were at it again, pushing past her defenses and diving into her soul. "There's something about you that—" he offered a wry smile "—that's comfortable."

Ava shouldn't be alone with Lucas in his room, but his gaze wouldn't let her go. "I'll be back later to vacuum."

"No." He blew out a noisy breath. "I don't mean to get in your way. I was leaving the hotel when I realized I forgot something." He lifted his briefcase off the floor and sat in the chair.

"How long are you staying in town?" The question escaped her mouth before she could stop it.

"It depends." He searched through the compartments in the case. "My stepmother banished me from celebrating the holidays with the family and my father took her side. I'm supposed to keep my distance until she cools off."

"Your father took her side?" Ava couldn't picture Lucas doing anything bad enough to be exiled. Granted, she'd known him less than twenty-four hours but he didn't seem like a man who intentionally stirred the pot.

"I recently connected with my biological father and his wife and sons are less than thrilled that I'm in the picture."

"I'm sorry."

Lucas moved to the bed and sat down then began taking things out of the briefcase. "It's fine." He looked at her. "I never expected them to roll out the welcome mat." The color of his eyes lost their intensity, looking like pieces of see-through blue glass. Lucas might say he didn't care, but Ava sensed his family's rejection had hurt.

"My parents were killed in a tornado when I was thirteen and I went into the foster care system." Why had she just blurted that out?

He stopped digging in the briefcase. "That's really young."

"That night I was staying with a friend across town." She dropped her gaze. "The storm leveled the trailer park we lived in but spared the rest of the community."

"Were your brothers or sisters hurt?"

"I was an only child."

"Me, too."

"Anyway, back to fickle families," she said. "My foster parents were great people and treated me like I was their real daughter. But things were a little rough in the beginning."

"How do you mean?"

"They already had a daughter and she didn't like me."

"Why?"

At first Ava had believed Julie was jealous of her because Ava was slim and pretty and popular in school. But later she figured out that wasn't it at all. "I got along with her father really well and she didn't." Ava shrugged. "My real dad and I were close. We did all the things a father and son would do together."

His gaze roamed over her. "I'm having a tough time picturing you carrying a hunting rifle and slinging a dead pheasant over your shoulder."

She laughed. "We didn't hunt but we went camping. And my father liked to build things. We made birdhouses together." She gazed into space remembering special times.

"Back to my foster father, he—"

"What was his name?"

This was the first time anyone had ever cared to know his name. "Ralph. But everyone called him Bud. Each night after supper he'd sit on the porch swing and wait for the sun to set. After Julie and I did the dishes, she'd go off with her friends and I'd sit on the swing with Bud. He could never replace my father but he was a good listener and I felt closer to my dad when we talked."

"Julie didn't like that."

Ava shook her head.

"I don't think my half brothers are jealous of me spending time with our father as much as they think I'm out to steal the family jewels."

"They sound spoiled."

"Yep. They grew up with the proverbial silver spoon shoved in their mouths and they have no concept of the meaning of hard work."

Ava raised a hand. "I think I know this story," she said. "Then you come along after being raised by a single mother and learning early in life that if you want to get ahead, you have to work hard."

Lucas grinned. "You're good."

"Both my parents worked before they were killed and even with two incomes money was always tight. When I was old enough to babysit, I began buying my own clothes. As soon as I turned sixteen, I got a job at a fast-food restaurant."

"I was paying my way early in life, too."

"Lucas, if you want a closer relationship with your father

ignore his wife and your brothers. Life is short and you never know what's around the corner." She knew that better than most after losing her parents at a young age and then her husband after two years of marriage.

"Are your foster parents still alive?"

"They passed away after I married." She flashed a sad smile. "I wish they'd lived long enough to meet my daughter. They would have loved Sophie."

Lucas's eyes widened and a twinge of disappointment pricked Ava that he hadn't smiled when he'd learned she was a mother. "Well," she said. "I have three more rooms to clean. I better get going."

"Ava."

She stopped in the doorway. "Yes?"

"How old is Sophie?"

"Four."

"Does she look like you?"

"We have the same color eyes and hair."

"I'd like to meet her sometime," he said.

Her heart melted. "Maybe you will." She closed the door behind her and wheeled the housekeeping cart to another room. What was the matter with her? She'd never shared those details of her life with anyone—not even Drew or Tilly.

Lucas is easy to talk to.

She'd better watch herself around the businessman or he'd slip past her defenses and put roots down in her heart before he left town.

LUCAS STARED AT the closed door after Ava left his room. He hadn't stopped thinking about her since last night. But in all of his thoughts never once had he imagined she was a mother.

It was only when Lucas's mom had become ill that he'd reflected more deeply about her role in his life. She'd always been there for him and he'd taken that for granted. He'd assumed all mothers were as strong as his—until they got sick. Then after she'd died he wondered if years of stress and struggling to get by had negatively impacted her health.

He thought of Ava working as a housekeeper at the hotel to support herself and her daughter. He pictured a cute little girl growing up without any extras like he had. No vacations or trips to the movies—places that cost money but gave kids memories of lifetime.

His cell phone buzzed with a text message from his father and his heart jumped in his chest. The little boy who'd grown up without a male role model yearned for unconditional love and acceptance but the grown man insisted all he cared about was respect and admiration.

Happy New Year, Lucas. I'm sorry things worked out the way they did. Enjoy your time in Montana.

Lucas took a moment to appreciate the fact that Roger had reached out to him, but the apology was harder to accept—his father could have confronted Claire and insisted Lucas didn't have to leave town, but he hadn't.

You have nothing to prove to Roger.

The thought startled Lucas. The adult in him acknowledged the truth in the statement, but there were two sides to every story and his mother had left a lot of questions unanswered before she'd died. Lucas hoped his hard work on behalf of Belfour Investments would earn Roger's trust and then maybe his father would open up about his relationship with Lucas's mother. He needed to understand the past in order to have the kind of father-son bond he'd always wished for.

He texted back a brief message then dropped the phone into his pocket, grabbed his jacket and left the room. When he reached the lobby, he stopped at the front desk. "Don't they ever give you a day off, Bob?"

"I wish, sir." He grinned. "What can I do for you?"

"I'm hoping you can tell me if anyone has turned in a flash drive." Lucas had fled the ballroom after kissing Ava and hadn't discovered the drive with his mother's diary entries was missing until he'd undressed for bed.

"I'll check the lost and found." Bob disappeared through the doorway behind the desk.

Lucas had a backup drive in his apartment in San Diego but that did him little good while he was in Marietta. Thankfully he'd memorized a few of the names on his mother's list.

"I'm sorry, sir," Bob said when he returned. "No flash drive."

"Thanks for checking."

"Of course."

Lucas stopped at the front doors where Ron stood sentry. "I thought you'd be home watching the college bowl games."

"I'm not a big football fan, sir."

As a result of growing up without a male role model Lucas wasn't an avid fan of any sport. However, thanks to his mother's love of soap operas, he could recall every twist and turn in the ongoing feud between Jill Abbott and Katherine Chancellor in *The Young and the Restless.*

Ron lowered his voice. "I'm surprising my wife with a Hawaiian vacation in February. I need all the overtime I can get."

"I've never been to Hawaii," Lucas said.

"Neither have we." Ron nodded to the icy parking lot. "Would you like me to bring your car around, sir?"

"Call me Lucas. We'll be seeing a lot of each other while I'm staying at the hotel."

"Yes, sir."

"I won't need the car," he said. "I'm walking."

"Sir, it's sixteen degrees out."

Lucas pulled on his leather gloves and fished a skullcap from his coat pocket. "I'll be fine."

"If you don't mind me asking, how far do you plan to walk?"

"I'm heading over to the Bramble House Bed and Breakfast."

Ron nodded. "Do you need directions to Bramble Lane?"

Lucas pulled out his cell phone. "I have the address in my GPS."

Ron held the door open. "Enjoy your stroll, sir."

"It's Lucas."

"Yes, sir."

Lucas decided to take a detour down Main Street before he headed over to Bramble Lane. Most of the businesses were closed on New Year's but that didn't matter. He wanted to get a look at Copper Mountain Chic and decide if the building—at least the outside—lived up to the judge's description. When he spotted the striped awning with the store name, he crossed the street to view the building from a distance.

There appeared to be at least two floors—possibly a third floor that might be an attic. The windows looked original— Mueller would love that. He pulled out his phone and took photos of the front then walked down the alley alongside the building and around to the back, taking more pictures. A Christmas wreath on the door at the top of the fire escape told him the second floor might have been converted into an apartment.

Excited about the property he texted Mueller and attached the photos then left the alley. When he reached the corner of Main and Court Streets his phone buzzed.

Mueller texted back that he was *very very* interested in the property. He asked Lucas for more details on the seller and said he'd do his own research on Marietta. Lucas was excited. If he snagged Mueller as a client, his half brothers couldn't question his loyalty.

By the time he reached Bramble Lane his face felt stiff and his eyes watered from the cold. The B&B was just down the block so he picked up the pace. As he drew closer he noticed the trees in the yard had been wrapped with holiday lights and more strands had been strung along the porch rail. An evergreen wreath hung on the door below the stained-glass transom and even though it wasn't porch-sitting weather, a pair of rocking chairs welcomed visitors.

A commotion down the block dragged his attention away from the Victorian home. An old man was walking his... Was that a *cat* on a leash? As the pair approached, he recognized the gentleman. "Judge Kingsley?" He smiled. "I don't know if you remember me, but—"

"Lucas Kendrick from San Diego. My wife is expecting you at her shop tomorrow morning."

"I took a few photos of the building. It's in great shape like you said."

"Sandra doesn't go half way on anything."

Lucas stared at the feline dressed in a Christmas pet sweater and green booties. "Who's your buddy?"

"Cat."

"His name is Cat?"

The judge nodded.

"I've never seen a cat walk on a leash."

The judge's scowl deepened. "Cat was living happily under my porch until my great-granddaughter showed up out of the blue one day and insisted the animal needed to lose weight."

"He doesn't look like he's enjoying his walk."

"Usually we don't make it out of the driveway." He turned around and tugged on the leash. Instead of following,

Cat lay down on the snow-packed sidewalk and tucked his legs under his body. "Stubborn stray." The judge pulled on the leash but the feline refused to stand.

"Maybe you should pick him up."

"I'd like to keep all of my fingers." The judge shuffled away, dragging Cat's body across the snow behind him. When he arrived at his driveway, Cat sprang off the ground, and the judge dropped the leash. The animal bolted into the yard and the old man followed, shaking his fist in the air.

Laughing, Lucas climbed the porch steps of the B&B. He'd thought about calling ahead and warning Mable Bramble he planned to stop by, but had nixed the idea. If she was too old to remember his mother, he hoped a personal visit would jar her memory.

"COME IN." THE blonde woman stepped aside and Lucas entered the Bramble B&B. "I'm Eliza Bramble. I've been expecting you."

She had? "Lucas Kendrick."

"I know," she said. "Ron phoned a few minutes ago and warned me that you were heading over here."

"I didn't realize one of the bellman's duties was to broadcast the whereabouts of the hotel guests."

Eliza shut the door after Lucas stepped into the foyer. "The staff worries that their out-of-state guests will underestimate the danger of our cold Montana temperatures."

"I'm looking for Mable Bramble."

"Mable is my great-aunt." She glanced past him into a parlor, where a gray-muzzled dog struggled to stand on the rug in front of the fireplace. "Stay, Ace." She sighed. "He's running out of gas in his old age, but he still likes to greet visitors when they enter the house."

Lucas went into the parlor and squatted before the dog. "You're a good boy." He scratched the mutt's ears, and the dog's tail thumped against the rug.

"There's a fresh pot of coffee on the sideboard in the dining room," Eliza said.

"That sounds good." Lucas returned to the foyer. "The sun's out but my face feels like a block of ice."

She laughed. "I bet when the temperature dips below sixty in San Diego, people turn on the heat."

"Did Ron tell you I was from California?"

She pointed to the radio on the table. As if on cue a song ended and the DJ's voice came on the air.

"This is KCMC country radio and I'm Dylan Morgan. It's time for the top of the hour update." Bells jingled in the background. "The New Year's ball at the Graff Hotel was a huge success. According to Big Sky Mavericks the fundraiser exceeded their expectations. Aside from the usual movers and shakers in Marietta, a hotel guest from San Diego, California, attended the event."

"Ron knows everyone in town. He gives Dylan the 411 on who comes and goes at the Graff." Eliza pointed to the rack in the corner. "Hang up your coat and I'll pour you a cup of coffee."

Lucas joined Eliza in the formal dining room and sat at

the table for twelve. "Thank you," he said when she handed him a mug.

"I bought a Keurig for the B&B, but Aunt Mable snubbed her nose at the machine, insisting the guests deserve coffee made the old-fashioned way."

He sampled the brew and closed his eyes. "Your aunt may be on to something. I have a Keurig in my apartment, but the coffee never tastes this good."

"Don't tell Aunt Mable. The next thing I know, she'll insist we swap out the Teflon frying pans for cast iron."

Lucas eyed the plate of pastries on the sideboard and Eliza placed the treats in front of him. "The guests finished breakfast hours ago then headed out to do some cross-country skiing."

He chose the jelly-filled donut, bit down hard and filling shot across the table. "Sorry." She handed him a napkin and he wiped up the mess.

"Who's your guest, Eliza?" A stern-looking woman entered the room, her shrewd gaze assessing Lucas.

"He's not my guest, Aunt Mable. He's yours."

Lucas swallowed the bite of pastry and stood. "Lucas Kendrick, ma'am."

Pencil-thin eyebrows arched over a pair of cloudy gray eyes. "I'm nobody's ma'am, young man." She waved him back to his seat then poured herself a cup of coffee.

As soon as the old woman sat, Eliza stood. "If you'll excuse me, I have work to do before the guests return tonight." She nodded to Lucas. "It was nice meeting you. Enjoy your stay in Marietta."

Left alone with Mable, Lucas smiled, hoping to thaw the chilly expression on the old woman's face. A roadmap of wrinkles covered the ashen skin, lines fanning out in multiple directions, some overlapping two or three times before vanishing into her steel-gray hair, which was pulled back in a tight bun. The severe style lifted the outer corner of her eyes, giving her a haughty air.

"Do I know you, young man?" she asked.

"No, Mrs. Bramble."

"Ms. Bramble. I never married."

He opened his mouth to apologize but thought better of it and took another bite of donut. "I believe you knew my mother."

"Don't you know better than to talk with your mouth full?"

"Sorry." He wiped the sugar crystals off his lips. "I was two when we left Marietta."

Mable pressed her palm to her chest. "Carol. Carol Kendrick."

"Yes." Lucas didn't know how old Mable was but he guessed late eighties like the judge. That she'd remembered his mom after all these years was a surprise.

"I see the resemblance now." Mable nodded. "You have Carol's blue eyes and dark lashes."

Boys had teased Lucas in elementary school, calling him a little girl because of his thick lashes. Things hadn't improved for him in high school when the girls in his classes accused him of wearing mascara.

Mable glanced at the doorway. "Did Carol come with

you?"

"Mom died of cancer two years ago."

"I'm very sorry."

"Mom didn't talk much about her life in Marietta," he said.

"Sometimes it's best to leave the past buried."

Lucas had a hunch the old woman was referring to herself.

"I was going through my mother's things not long ago, and I came across a note she'd written." He sipped his coffee. "She'd hoped to one day return to Marietta and thank the people who helped us." He nodded. "Your name was at the top of the list."

Mable's eyes widened.

"She'd also written down that she owed you fifty dollars." Lucas took out the fifty-dollar bill he'd put in his wallet before he'd gotten on the plane yesterday.

Mable stared at the money.

"Please accept the payment," Lucas said. "It would have meant a lot to my mother to know that her debts had been paid."

Fingers bent with arthritis folded the bill in half and slid it into the pocket of her sweater.

"Would you mind telling me how you helped my mother?"

"I didn't do much, young man."

"I'd still like to know."

"Give me one of those." She nodded to the donuts.

Lucas pushed the platter toward her, guessing the dowager needed a hit of sugar for courage. She nibbled the pastry and he waited patiently for her to speak.

"The busybodies in Marietta call me Ms. Congeniality." Her eyes narrowed. "It's not a compliment."

Lucas pinched his thumb and forefinger together. "You must be a tiny bit friendly if you helped my mom."

"Are you going to talk or let me?"

Mable was almost as old as the first box of Girl Scout cookies but her mouth fired off faster than a modern-day tweet. "Please continue."

"Years ago I met with a group of ladies every Thursday. It was the first week in November when I spotted your mother waiting at the bus stop on my way to tea. She looked like a ragamuffin." Mable bit off another bite of donut, making Lucas wait again for her to continue. "When I left Eleanor's house three hours later, Carol was still sitting at the stop. It had begun to snow and she wasn't wearing a cap or gloves."

"You felt sorry for her."

Mable snorted. "Hardly, young man. Life is full of disappointments and not even those with fame or fortune are spared."

Someone in Mable's past had hurt her—maybe a man—and had left her bitter and jaded.

"Back to your mother," she said. "A young runaway is not what the Marietta Chamber of Commerce wants visitors to see on their way into town."

Ouch.

"The Brambles were one of the first families to settle in

Marietta in 1879. Generation after generation worked diligently to clear out the riffraff and civilize this town."

Mable had considered his mother riffraff?

"I brought Carol home with me and insisted she take a proper bath and clean up."

"I'm sure she appreciated your hospitality."

"I said she couldn't stay long." Mable sighed. "I told her I wasn't running a home for wayward girls." While she finished her donut, Lucas fetched himself a refill on his coffee then topped off Mable's cup before returning to his chair.

"It wasn't until your mother removed her coat that I noticed she was expecting. Naturally I felt obligated to feed her. She ate scrambled eggs and toast then I sent her to bed."

Lucas's mom must have made a big impact if the old lady remembered what food she'd cooked that day.

"While Carol slept, I made a few inquiries around town, hoping to find a place that would take her in, but we didn't have any organizations back then that helped teenagers in distress."

"So you let her stay with you."

A crooked finger wiggled in the air. "Just until the baby...*you* were born. I made sure she remained inside the house. No one in my family even knew she was here." Mable frowned. "Don't give me that look, young man. If people had discovered I was helping Carol, I'd have had charities and nonprofits beating down my door for donations."

"Did my mom say why she was at the bus stop?"

"She'd arrived a few days earlier but had to leave the

place she'd been staying. She said it wasn't safe there anymore."

"Where was that?"

"I didn't ask and she didn't say."

"What did she do after I was born?"

"By the time you were here, I'd convinced Virginia Pritchard, the owner of the Main Street Diner, to give Carol a job."

Virginia's name was another one Lucas recalled from his mother's list.

"She and her husband Herb sold the diner years ago and moved to Billings. I believe Herb bought a bar there."

"I was hoping I'd have a chance to introduce myself to Mrs. Pritchard."

"She and Herb are in town visiting family. Virginia usually stops by the diner every day."

"When did my mother move into the Sunset Apartments?"

"After she left the hospital with you. I paid the first two months rent and the security deposit for her."

"That was generous."

"She had to go somewhere and I couldn't very well have her living here." Mable sipped her coffee. "At the time the carriage house on the property was filled with old furniture and decades of family possessions. I hired two neighborhood boys to move a few necessities into the apartment."

"Necessities?"

"A bed, dresser, kitchen supplies and a table."

It sounded as if she'd furnished the apartment. "Did I

sleep in a crib or on the floor?"

Mable brushed at imaginary crumbs on her sweater. "I gave your mother an old family cradle."

An heirloom. "Did she return the cradle?"

"Of course."

"Is the fifty dollars what my mother owned you for the rent and deposit you put down on the apartment?"

"Carol paid me ten dollars a month until she left town." The spinster pursed her mouth. "She disappeared without giving her notice at the diner."

Lucas felt bad. Despite her grumpy disposition, Mable had cared about them and his mom had hurt her feelings when she'd taken off without saying goodbye.

"My mother returned to San Diego," he said.

Mable studied a scratch in the table. "She never talked about her family."

"Mom was born and raised in San Diego. When she became pregnant with me, her parents disowned her. One of the notes she'd written said that we had to leave Marietta before it was too late."

"What did she mean too late?"

"She said the town and its people were becoming our family and if we didn't leave then we never would."

"If she liked it here it doesn't make sense that she'd leave."

"She hoped that once her parents saw me, they'd take her back."

"Did they?"

"No." Lucas had never met his grandparents. And his

mother hadn't gone to their funerals when they'd passed away.

"And your father?" Mable asked.

Lucas shook his head. "We were on our own."

"That's terrible."

"I reached out to my dad after my mom passed away."

"Oh?"

"I work for him now." He answered the question in Mable's eyes. "Belfour Real Estate Investments."

"Do have a young lady in your life?"

Ava came to mind and he smiled. "I'm working on it." He pushed his chair back and stood. "I've taken up enough of your time."

"How long will you be in town?" she asked.

"I'm not sure. A week." Maybe longer if anything developed between him and Ava.

Mable's fingernail tapped the table. "I don't know why Carol felt compelled to thank me again. She'd already thanked me numerous times."

"Did you see her often after I was born?"

"I stopped at the diner for coffee once in a while."

The Graff was more Mable's speed. "I'd like to add my thanks to my mother's," he said.

"What for?"

"Because of you, Virginia and a handful of other folks in this town, my mom decided to raise me herself and not give me up for adoption."

"I didn't know that Carol had considered adoption." It might have been the lighting in the room but Lucas swore the old woman's eyes shimmered with tears. "Take care, young man."

"You also." Lucas went into the foyer and shrugged into his winter coat then stepped outside. He put on his hat and gloves then walked back to the hotel, wearing a smile on his face as he envisioned his teenage mother being hen-pecked by dowager Bramble.

Chapter Four

A VA PACED BETWEEN the racks of dresses, waiting for Sandra to arrive at the shop to discuss her business proposal. She'd left the door to the upstairs apartment open because Sophie would be down in a minute after she watched her TV program. Ava stopped and faced the front of the store. Her gaze landed on the tattered leather chair in the display window.

Sandra had draped a sequined dress across the armrest and fanned the material out to cover the split in the seat cushion. Despite its sad state of neglect the chair was an eye stopper with copper detailing on the legs and across the top. A brass plate had been screwed down at the end of one arm, but the etching was illegible.

Ava went over to the chair and smoothed out a wrinkle in the dress then sniffed the air. She swore she smelled tobacco. She inhaled again but the odor had vanished.

The bells on the door jingled and Sandra entered the store. "Sorry, I'm late."

"No worries." Ava pointed to the chair. "I thought you'd planned to restore the seat cushion."

"I decided to leave it as it is." Sandra removed her coat and gloves. "If chairs could talk, I believe this one would have quite a story." Her eyebrows formed a V above her nose.

"What's the matter?" Ava asked.

"I was sure I draped that dress over the other arm of the chair." She rearranged the garment. "Much better."

Sophie's steps echoed on the back stairs and her daughter entered the shop. Sandra bent down and gave her a hug. "How's my little angel?"

"Good. Aunt Sandra, can I draw on your pretty papers?"

"You sure can." Sandra took Sophie's hand and led her behind the sales counter then placed her on the stool. Ava and Sophie had grown close to Sandra after they'd moved into the upstairs apartment. The businesswoman didn't have any children of her own. She had a close bond with the judge's granddaughter-in-law and great-granddaughter, and she treated Sophie like a grandchild and Ava like a daughter.

"Here's your box." Sandra set the colorful craft container on the counter. She'd purchased the supplies for Sophie to play with when she and Ava came down to visit in the store.

"I'm gonna make you a heart card." Sophie pushed her glasses up her nose.

"I would love a heart card." Sandra smiled at Ava. "I need coffee."

"We'll be in the back room, honey." Ava followed Sandra into the break room, which was also used to store extra inventory.

Sandra removed her coat and hung it on an antique stand then said, "Sit down and tell me what's happening."

Ava had shared her plans for the co-op with Sandra

months ago because she'd wanted the businesswoman's input and had looked to her as a mentor. "I still haven't found an affordable place to rent for the resale shop."

"Do you need a loan to get the project off the ground?"

"I appreciate the offer, but I'm not asking for a loan."

Sandra was independently wealthy. Her family had been involved in industrial mining for decades and she'd inherited millions when her parents had passed away. And then her first husband had been a successful banker and had left Sandra another small fortune when he'd died. Sandra had purchased the building and opened her clothing boutique to keep busy, not because she needed to make a living.

"Remember when we talked right before Thanksgiving? You said the judge wanted you to get rid of the dress shop so that the two of you could spend more time together?"

Sandra grimaced. "I didn't think he was that serious, but he brought it up again at the ball Sunday night."

Sandra was fifteen years younger than the judge and was twice as active. She'd told Ava that running a business made her feel useful.

"I have a proposal that I believe will benefit both of us." Ava leaned forward.

"I assume we're still talking about the co-op?"

Ava's final semester project in college had been to create a co-op—on paper. Since Sandra was a businesswoman and her landlord, Ava had asked her for input on the project. Last spring after she'd graduated Ava had decided to turn her co-op into a reality, but she'd yet to find a location in town willing to rent a space she could afford.

"I've been mulling over your suggestion that the co-op resale shop needs a theme. I don't want customers believing the items we sell can be found at any garage sale."

Sandra sipped her coffee. "Did you decide on a theme?"

"The women and I discussed it, and we've decided to specialize in refurbished vintage furniture and décor."

Sandra's eyes lit up. "That's a fabulous idea. You know I love anything vintage. What made you choose that?"

"The display window out front. There's something about that shabby chair that calls to me."

Sandra laughed. "You can't have it back."

This past September while working at the hotel Ava had helped the events director, Walker Wilder, push the chair down a hallway to the freight elevator. Walker had told Ava that she was returning the chair to the attic. Knowing how much Sandra loved vintage furniture, Ava had asked the manager of the Graff if he'd consider donating the chair to Sandra's shop and he'd let Ava take it.

"What's this proposition that benefits both of us?"

"I'm proposing a partnership that would require no investment on your end." Ava held up her hand. "You don't have to give me an answer right away. I just want you to mull it over for a little while."

"Okay." Sandra nodded.

"The women in the co-op would use the basement of this building as a work room where they'd refurbish the items we sell in the store. This room—" Ava swept her arm in front of her "—will be the store where we sell our items to the public. There's plenty of parking in the alley and customers can enter through the back door so they wouldn't disturb the dress shop."

Sandra looked as if she was going to ask a question, so Ava rushed on. "The other room—" she pointed to a door that led into a smaller storage area, but also contained a bathroom "—will be turned into a childcare room so the mothers in the co-op can bring their kids with them while they're working in the basement or here in store."

Sandra's eyebrow arched. "If you're proposing a partnership and you don't want any money from me, then I assume I wouldn't be charging you rent for using the basement or the two rooms back here."

"But—" Ava held up a finger "—in lieu of paying rent, our co-op members, me included, will manage your store when you're traveling with the judge." Ava spread her arms wide. "You get the best of both worlds. You keep your business and you keep your husband happy because you're able to spend more time with him." She smiled. "It's a win-win for both of us."

Sandra's manicured nail tapped against the table. "I'm definitely intrigued."

"And as a bonus," Ava said, "you can use any of the vintage items in our store to decorate the dress shop."

"That is a bonus."

Ava gave herself a mental pat on the back. Decorating with refurbished items was a brilliant way to advertise the co-op. Sandra sold upscale clothing and her customers had money to spend. If the women liked the décor they saw on display in the shop, Sandra could send the ladies and their checkbooks to the back room to browse more merchandise.

"Ava, I'm impressed. But before I can give this proposal serious consideration I need to run this by my lawyer."

"I'll go upstairs right now and make a copy of the paperwork."

Sandra's phone went off. "I need to take this call, dear."

Ava left Sandra in the break room and went out front. "Honey, Aunt Sandra's on the phone and I have to run upstairs for something. Be right back."

"Okay."

Ava climbed the back stairs to the apartment and went into the bedroom where her filing cabinet doubled as a nightstand. She pulled out the co-op folder and made a copy of the plan on the printer. She hurried back to the stairs but froze on the first step when she heard a masculine voice in the dress shop.

"Good morning, young lady."

Hadn't Sandra locked the front door after she'd come into the store early?

"Is your grandmother around?"

The voice sounded familiar but Ava had trouble placing it.

"Nana's not here but Aunt Sandra's back there."

Ava envisioned Sophie pointing to the storeroom behind the checkout counter.

"What's your name?" Sophie asked.

"Lucas Kendrick."

Lucas?

Maybe Angelica is playing matchmaker.

"I'm Sophie. Wanna see my picture?"

"Sure."

Sophie wasn't used to being around men—her daughter had no memory of her father and Ava hadn't dated anyone since Drew.

When Ava had told Lucas she had a daughter, he'd seemed surprised and she was curious to how he'd respond to Sophie.

"Your glasses are falling off your nose," he said.

"Mommy says it's 'cause I have a little face."

"Is that Cinderella?" he asked.

"And her pumpkin coach."

"I thought Cinderella's hair was brown."

Sophie giggled. "No, silly. Cinderella has yellow hair."

"Are you sure? I think I saw Cinderella the other night at the ball and she had a brown ponytail."

Ava's heart swooned.

"You saw Cinderella?" Sophie asked.

"I sure did, princess."

Sophie giggled. "I'm not a princess."

"You look like a princess. All you need is a sparkly crown."

"I have a princess dress in my toy box."

Sophie had picked out the costume to wear on Halloween this past fall and then she'd worn the dress over flannel PJ's to bed for several weeks after.

"Maybe you're a princess and you don't know it," Lucas said.

"I'm gonna ask my mom if I'm a princess when she gets

here."

Sophie's comment reminded Ava that she was eaves-dropping but she was reluctant to interrupt them when Sophie was enjoying his attention.

"How old are you?" Lucas asked.

"Four. How old are you?"

Ava smiled. Kids had no filter.

"Thirty," he said.

"My mommy's twenty-six. Do you have a little girl?"

"I don't."

"Why not?"

"That's a good question. I don't know."

"You should have a little girl," Sophie said. "Nana says girls don't make messes like boys."

"I'll keep that in mind." After a few moments of silence, Lucas spoke again. "There sure are a lot of fancy dresses in here."

The stool behind the counter scraped against the floor then Ava heard the click-clack of her daughter's shoes. "Wanna see my favorite dress?"

"Sure."

"It's got lots of sparkles."

Ava pictured the dress Sophie was showing Lucas. The blush-colored material had hundreds of sequins sewn around the waistband and puffed sleeves.

"That looks like a princess dress," he said. "What about this one for me?"

"Boys don't wear dresses." Sophie's reply made Ava smile.

"Hello, Lucas," Sandra's voice carried up the stairs. "I didn't hear you come in."

Wait a minute. How did Ava's landlord know Lucas?

"I forgot you were coming this morning," Sandra said.

Forgot? Why was Lucas here? Ava started down the stairs.

"Princess Sophie and I have been discussing the latest fashion trends in the Marietta kingdom."

Ava stepped through the doorway behind the counter and smiled when Lucas looked her way. His eyes widened then his gaze dropped to Sophie before returning to Ava's face.

"I see you've met my daughter," she said.

Lucas smiled. "You didn't tell me she was a princess."

Ava walked over and handed Sandra the copy of the co-op proposal then she brushed her daughter's bangs off her forehead. "Honey, go put your drawings away. It's almost time to leave for preschool."

After Sophie walked off, Sandra glanced between Lucas and Ava. "You two know each other?"

"We met at the New Year's Eve ball," Ava said. Then she repeated Sandra's question. "How do you know Lucas?"

"I met Sandra's husband, Alistair, at the hotel."

Ava recalled seeing Lucas sitting by the judge at a card table.

"I love the store," Lucas said. "The brick interior and exposed copper piping on the ceiling is exactly what my client is looking for."

Client? Ava touched Sandra's arm. "What's going on?"

Sandra bit down on her lip. "Alistair told Lucas I was

interested in selling and Lucas wanted to see the building. I suggested he drop by this morning."

Ava's gaze swung to Lucas. "You're not here to see me?"

He rocked back on his heels. "I didn't know you lived here."

"Ava rents the upstairs apartment," Sandra said.

Lucas glanced between the women. "If this is a bad time, I can return later."

Sandra rolled the co-op proposal into a tube then tapped it against her palm. Ava wished she understood why her landlord appeared so distressed. The bell on the door jingled again and the judge strolled in.

"Lucas," Alistair said. "I'm glad to see you made it." The men shook hands, and then Alistair smiled at his wife. "Has he persuaded you to sell yet?"

Ava stared at Sandra. "I thought—"

"Sandra said she'd sell the building if I took her on a trip around the world." The judge pulled two plane tickets out of his coat pocket. "I'm calling her bluff."

When the blood drained from Sandra's face, Ava grasped her arm and escorted her behind the sales counter. Once the older woman was sitting down, Ava spoke to her daughter. "Sophie, run upstairs and get our coats." Then she whispered, "Did you know Alistair was going to buy plane tickets?"

Sandra shook her head.

"My wife's worried about selling," the judge said to Lucas, "because she doesn't want the building to fall into the hands of someone who won't take care of it."

Sandra tugged Ava's sleeve. "I had to tell him something, so he'd stop pestering me."

The judge approached the counter. "Did you ask Lucas what his client would do with the building if he bought it?"

"You interrupted us before he had a chance to tell me," Sandra said.

Lucas approached the counter and grabbed a pen from the decorative holder then scribbled on the back of a business card. "His name is Stan Mueller. If you do an Internet search on him, you'll see all the properties he's developed."

"What kind of properties?" Sandra said.

"Stan turns historic buildings into high-end condos and apartments. He's done projects out west as well as cities on both coasts. You can rest assured he'll keep the integrity and beauty of this building intact."

Sandra nodded. "I'll need to look into Mr. Mueller."

"Don't waste any time," the judge said. "We're starting the first leg of our journey in Australia at the end of the month."

Sandra's mouth dropped open.

"What do you say we grab a cup of coffee across the street, Lucas?" Alistair winked at Sandra. "I'll give you a few pointers on how to win my wife over."

Before the men made it to the door, Ava called out, "Are you free for lunch today, Lucas?"

He smiled. "I am."

"There's a café down the block. I'll meet you there at eleven-thirty," she said.

Lucas nodded to Sandra. "I'll be in touch."

As soon as the door closed behind the men, Sandra gripped Ava's arms. "What am I going to do? I don't want to sell, but Alistair bought plane tickets." Tears filled Sandra's eyes. "Ava, he's terrified of flying. He must really want this for us."

"There's no need to panic yet." Ava wasn't sure if her words were meant to convince Sandra or herself. "Talk to your lawyer and then we'll chat again about my proposal."

In the meantime, Ava would meet Lucas for lunch and explain that he'd have to find a different property for his client. He was a reasonable man. He'd understand.

⤜⤜⤜⤛⤛⤛

LUCAS WAS WAITING inside Java Café at a table by the window when Ava entered the business. He stood and pulled out a chair for her as she approached the table. She could get used to being around a man with manners. "Thank you," she said.

"Where's Sophie?" he asked.

"I pick her up from preschool in an hour."

"That's too bad. I was looking forward to chatting with the princess."

"You made quite an impression on her." Sophie had talked non-stop on the way to preschool. Ava smiled at the thought that the man sitting across from her could cast a spell on females from four years old to seventy and every age in between.

A waitress delivered glasses of water to the table. "Do you

folks know what you want?"

Ava looked at Lucas. "The club sandwich is good. I think I'll have that, please."

"Same for me, thanks," he said.

The pencil paused on the order pad. "Coleslaw or fries?"

"Fries," they said at the same time then laughed.

"Anything else to drink?"

"Just water for me," Ava said.

Lucas nodded. "Water's fine."

"Comin' right up."

Once they were alone, Lucas said, "Your daughter looks just like you."

"She's my pride and joy."

"Did you have to wear glasses when you were little?"

"Yes. I had Lasik surgery a few years ago to correct my sight."

"Sophie said she's four. And you're twenty-six?"

"That's right."

He nodded. "I'm thirty."

She almost said *I know* before she caught herself and had to explain she'd eavesdropped on his and Sophie's conversation in Sandra's shop. While they waited for their food, they chatted about the weather, the businesses on Main Street—neither mentioning the dress shop.

"Will there be anything else?" their server asked.

Lucas nodded to Ava and she shook her head. "I think we're good, thank you." Left alone again, he said, "I had no idea you were the tenant living in the apartment above Sandra's store."

"My boss, Angelica, used to rent from Sandra. When she moved into the housekeeper's quarters at the hotel, Sophie and I took over the apartment."

He set his sandwich on the plate. "Ava, I don't want you to worry about being kicked out of your home if Sandra sells the building. I'd advocate on your behalf to see that you and Sophie can continue to rent the upstairs unit. And if he won't agree to that then I'll tell him the deal's off the table."

Ava stared at her plate, not wanting Lucas to see how much his words meant to her. They'd just met but his sincerity tempted her to trust him. His compassion and worry for her and Sophie made her feel awful because she intended to thwart his plans.

"I never expected an opportunity like this to land in my lap," he said.

"About that opportunity." Ava tried to arrange her thoughts into coherent sentences. "The judge might have misled you a little when he said Sandra was waiting for the right buyer to come along before she let go of the building."

Lucas nodded. "I can tell she's nervous about selling the building." He glanced out the window. "I'm not a superstitious person but I feel like my whole life had been building up to this trip." His mouth curved in a wry smile. "It's as if I was destined to be here at this point in time."

Ava swirled a French fry in the puddle of ketchup on her plate. If what Lucas said was true, why couldn't destiny have waited a few more months—until after she and Sandra had become business partners?

"I feel like the key to finding my place in life and with

my family, is here in Marietta." He grimaced. "That sounds really stupid, doesn't it?"

"Not at all." Ava couldn't remember ever having a conversation like this with Drew. He never reflected on the past or the future. He'd focused on the here and now and he'd never been interested in hearing Ava's dreams. "What do you mean by finding your place with your family?"

"My brothers don't trust me. They believe I want to get even with Roger because he'd abandoned me and my mom."

"What made you decide to contact him?" Ava asked.

"My mother urged me to before she died."

Her heart ached when she envisioned Lucas sitting at his mom's bedside holding her hand, promising her anything in hopes of keeping her alive a little longer.

"I never knew the details of what happened between my parents but I blamed my father because he wasn't there. A few months after my mother died, I couldn't stop wondering why she'd wanted me to connect with him."

"So you decided to follow through with her request."

"I'd convinced myself that I wasn't going to like him." Lucas drew in a deep breath and blew it out slowly.

"What happened?"

"I applied for a job at his company and was invited to his office. We shook hands. We were both polite, but there was something in his eyes when he looked at me." Lucas shook his head. "The only word I can come up with to describe it is *relief.* Then he offered me a job."

"Wait a minute," she said. "He just took your word that you were his son? He didn't demand a DNA test?"

"My half brothers wanted proof but my father said it wasn't necessary. In the end we both took a DNA test and it settled the issue." Lucas stared out the window, the muscle along his jaw bunching. When he finally turned away, her breath caught at the shiny film over his eyes. "I accepted the job because even after not being a part of his life all these years, I wanted to make him proud of me." Lucas cleared his throat. "I've been on a mission since I began working at Belfour Investments to find a way to make a positive impact in the company and prove to my half brothers that I belong there as much as they do."

"I'm sure your father appreciates your dedication," Ava said.

"He does, but…" Lucas chuckled. "I'm hogging the conversation."

"That's okay," she said. "Yesterday we talked about me when I mentioned my foster father." She dipped her head. "Finish your thought."

"Belfour Real Estate Investments is a successful but small company. Making a deal with a developer as well-known and respected as Stan Mueller would potentially open doors to more lucrative business deals."

Ava's stomach grew queasy. Lucas didn't have to tell her the rest—she could see it in his eyes. Making a business deal with Stan Mueller would prove Lucas's devotion to the family business. And after growing up without a father, he wanted to make Roger Belfour proud.

"Sandra's building has a unique history and it was pure luck that the judge mentioned it to me," he said. "It almost feels surreal that I'd have an opportunity like this so soon after taking a position at my father's firm." He grasped Ava's hand and squeezed. "I've got to figure out a way to make this happen before I leave town."

Before I leave town. Ava had been drawn in by Lucas's story but he'd just reminded her that he was here for the short-term and she was in Marietta for the long-term. Although she was sympathetic to his situation, she had to look out for her own interests. And before he got too carried away with trying to buy Sandra's building, she needed him to know there was more standing in his way than negotiating Ava's rent with the developer.

She checked her phone. Time had gotten away from them. She had to pick Sophie up from preschool in fifteen minutes. "What are you doing for dinner tonight?"

"I don't have any plans." He smiled. "Would you and Sophie like to have dinner with me at the hotel?"

"No, thank you." She laughed. "I spend enough time working there."

"I could take you somewhere else."

She shook her head. "Come over to the Moore Apartment des Spaghettis at six-thirty."

"Did I mention I love Italian food?" He signaled for the check.

The waitress dropped the bill on the table as she passed by and Lucas snatched it.

"I invited you to lunch," she said. "I'm paying."

"You're making dinner tonight."

Ava thought about the bomb she planned to drop on

him later, and felt even guiltier that he was covering the bill. Maybe she would stop by the bakery on the way home this afternoon and buy something sweet for dessert to soften the blow.

Chapter Five

"YOU'RE SQUEAKY CLEAN now," Ava said helping Sophie dry off after her bath.

"When is Mr. Lucas gonna be here?"

"In less than an hour." Ava helped her daughter into her pink footie pajamas. "Tomorrow is garbage day. Will you please bring me the trash can in your bedroom?"

Sophie took off running through the apartment and Ava cleaned up the bathroom then returned to the kitchen and retrieved a trash bag from the pantry. She stood in Sophie's bedroom doorway and held the bag open while her daughter dumped the contents of the wastebasket inside. "Thank you."

"Is Mr. Lucas gonna read me a bedtime story?"

"If you ask him nicely, I'm sure he will. Why don't you pick out a book while I take the trash to the Dumpster?" Ava went into the bathroom and emptied the can beneath the sink. Before she tied the bag closed, she spotted the black flash drive she'd found on the hotel ballroom floor and the gadget brought back the memory of Lucas's kiss. She emptied the basket beneath the desk in her bedroom then tugged the strings closed and set the bag by the back door while she stuck her sock feet into her snow boots and put on her coat and mittens.

It had begun snowing—just flurries—an hour ago, making the stairs on the fire escape slick. When she reached the ground the wind picked up and she hurried across the pavement. The weather report called for overnight flurries but the snow hitting her face was wet and heavy. When she reached the metal container, the lid was already open so she flung the bag inside and then reached behind the unit and pushed the lid up and over the bin.

By the time she'd climbed the stairs to the landing the snow was falling even harder. Hopefully they'd get no more than a couple of inches by morning. When she entered the warm apartment she kicked off her boots, hung up her coat and then went to the stove to stir the sauce.

Sophie joined her in the kitchen and climbed onto a stool at the island. "I'm hungry, Mommy."

"I bet you are." They usually ate dinner around five. Ava placed a small serving of grapes in front of her daughter.

"I wanna go ice-skating."

"I'm not working this Saturday. I'll take you then." Ava slid a loaf of French bread into the oven then checked the three place settings on the bistro table, making sure she hadn't forgotten anything.

A knock on the door sent Sophie dashing across the room. "Mr. Lucas is here!" Her daughter flung the door open, and a squall of cold wind traveled through the room, carrying Lucas's chuckle on a carpet of ice crystals.

"Well, hello there, Princess Sophie." Lucas glanced at Ava and smiled, the gesture lighting up his killer blue eyes.

He held a bottle of wine and a small gift bag in one hand.

She returned his smile. "Come in."

He closed the door behind him.

Sophie slid her hand into Lucas's and said, "Wanna see the book I picked out for you to read to me?"

Ava's throat tightened as she stared at Lucas's big hand clinging to her daughter's tiny fingers. Sophie didn't warm up to people quickly but the way she interacted with Lucas told Ava that he'd snuck past her daughter's defenses in record time.

"Wait until after supper, Sophie. Show Mr. Lucas where he can hang his coat."

Sophie pointed to the hooks on the wall by the door then went back to the island and climbed onto the stool. "I'm eating grapes."

Lucas wandered closer and peered at the fruit. "I thought princesses only ate cake and candy."

Sophie shook her head and popped a grape into her mouth.

Lucas set the bottle of red wine on the counter and then put the gift bag in front of Sophie. "I saw this today and thought of you."

Her daughter's eyes widened and Ava nodded that it was okay to accept the gift.

Sophie squealed. "Look, Mommy, it's a princess crown." She held up the silver tiara with colored plastic jewels.

"Let's see if it fits." Lucas took the crown and placed it on Sophie's head making a show of positioning it just right.

"It's lovely," Ava said, turning away from the tender scene. She wished he hadn't brought the gift or the wine, especially in light of her reason for inviting him to dinner.

"I hope you don't mind if we eat right away," Ava said. "Sophie's bedtime is seven-thirty."

Lucas peered into the pot on the stove. This was the first time she'd had a man in her apartment and until now the place had always felt roomy.

"It smells great," he said.

Ava thought so, too, when she caught a whiff of his cologne.

"What can I do to help?"

"You can pour Sophie a glass of milk and the wine opener is in that drawer." She pointed to the end of the counter. "Glasses are in the cupboard over there."

Ava made quick work of straining the noodles then mixing them with the sauce. She placed the warmed bread on the table and then dished out three servings of spaghetti before sitting down.

While they ate, Lucas entertained Sophie with stories of his adventures as a kid growing up near the ocean, playing pretend pirates with his friends when the big ships and tankers came into port. And he told tales of sneaking up on the walruses and otters sunning themselves on the rocks. Then he taught Sophie how to make walrus sounds and her daughter laughed so hard she snorted milk through her nose.

When Sophie yawned, Ava said, "Go brush your teeth, honey, then Mr. Lucas can read you a story while I clean up the kitchen."

Sophie hurried into the bathroom, closing the door loudly behind her.

Ava began clearing the table and Lucas helped her carry the dishes to the sink.

"Thank you," he said. "The food was great."

She believed him because he'd had two servings and three pieces of bread. "You're welcome."

"I'm done!" Sophie burst from the bathroom and raced to her bedroom door. "C'mon, Mr. Lucas."

He chuckled then whispered for Ava's ears only, "I didn't realize princesses were so impatient." He followed her daughter into the bedroom.

"What book are we reading, Princess Sophie?"

"Cinderella."

Ava stared at the empty doorway, taken aback by how emotionally off-balance she'd felt around Lucas. She hadn't expected him to focus so much attention on Sophie and Ava had never seen her daughter act this animated. That he would be the first man to read her daughter a story seemed fitting. She loaded the dishwasher, listening to Lucas's deep voice echo through the apartment, filling all the empty spaces.

"Once upon a time there was a beautiful princess called Sophie."

"No, silly, it's Cinderella!"

"Cinderella had two ugly stepsisters who were very unkind and made her do all the hard work."

"I don't have any sisters. Do you, Mr. Lucas?"

"Nope. But you know what?"

"What?"

"I have two half brothers."

Ava set the dishrag in the sink then went to the doorway and peeked inside the room. Sophie sat in the middle of the bed, holding her stuffed bear, her big eyes fixed on Lucas.

"Do your brothers make you do all the work?"

"Sometimes." Lucas gently pushed Sophie's glasses up her nose. "They keep slipping."

"Mommy fixed 'em but they broke again."

"Can I try?" Sophie handed her glasses to Lucas and he squeezed the wire bridge between his fingers then slid them on her face.

"How's that? Better?"

"I think so," Sophie said.

"Shake your head." Sophie obeyed, giggling. The glasses had stayed on.

"You fixed 'em, Mr. Lucas!" She rolled onto her knees and hugged him around the neck.

The tender scene brought tears to Ava's eyes. Little girls needed their daddies and her daughter had never known that feeling of security that only fathers could give their children.

"Back to the story," he said. "Cinderella had to sweep the floors and wash the dishes while her sisters dressed in fine clothes and went to parties."

"Mommy went to a ball but she said there wasn't gonna be any princes."

"Sometimes princes show up when you least expect them."

Ava pressed her hand against her thumping heart.

"When Cinderella arrived at the ball, she looked so beautiful that everyone asked who she was," Lucas said, "even—"

"The ugly sisters," Sophie said.

"You finish the story."

"The prince and Cinderella danced until the clock struck midnight." Sophie sucked in a loud breath and rushed on. "Cinderella ran down the steps but her glass slipper fell off."

"Then what happened?" he asked.

"The golden coach turned into a pumpkin and the horses turned back into mice."

"And Cinderella's driver?"

"He turned into a rat. Eww!"

Lucas chuckled.

"Then Cinderella walked home and sat by the fire until her mean sisters came home from the ball."

"I bet Cinderella didn't have to do chores for much longer, did she?"

"No, 'cause the prince put the glass slipper on Cinderella's foot and it fit."

"And the prince and Cinderella lived happily ever after," he said.

"No, silly, the prince and Cinderella got married."

"I forgot. They have to get married before they can live happily ever after," Lucas said.

Ava stepped farther into the room. "Time for bed, honey. Thank Mr. Lucas for reading to you."

"Thank you, Mr. Lucas."

"You're welcome, Princess Sophie."

Her daughter crawled beneath the covers and Ava took a step forward, intending to adjust the quilt, but Lucas beat her to the punch. He removed Sophie's glasses and set them on the nightstand then he make a big production of pulling the blanket up to her chin and tucking it around her body until she looked like a little mummy. "Snug as a bug in a rug," he said.

Sophie giggled. "I can't move."

Lucas loosened the blanket. "Better?" Sophie nodded and he turned out the light. "Sweet dreams, Princess Sophie."

"Mr. Lucas?"

"What?"

"Are you gonna be here in the morning?"

Lucas smiled. "Tonight I will return to my room at the castle Graff."

Sophie smiled. "Bye, Mr. Lucas."

"Bye, Princess Sophie." Lucas moved past Ava in the doorway, his chest brushing against her arm.

"I'll be right out," she said.

"I like Mr. Lucas, Mommy. Can he be our friend?"

"Mr. Lucas doesn't live in Marietta. His home is far away."

"Can we go live where Mr. Lucas lives?"

Her daughter already had a crush on Lucas and Ava was following in her footsteps. "No, honey. We can't leave Nana all alone in Marietta."

Ava wanted to believe Sophie would feel this way about any man who paid attention to her, but there was something special about Lucas. After living with Drew's macho bluster, Lucas's gentle nature and kindness were a breath of fresh air.

"Nana can come with us to Mr. Lucas's house," Sophie

said.

"Nana loves Marietta. And we love Nana," Ava said. "We're a family and family sticks together." And Lucas's family was in San Diego. Fate, karma or kismet may have brought him to Marietta but she doubted their powers were strong enough to hold him here.

LUCAS WAITED IN the kitchen for Ava to say good night to her daughter. The little girl was a heart-stealer with her big brown eyes, made even larger by the magnifying lenses of her glasses.

Family sticks together.

Ava's words rang through Lucas's head. Life had taught him that traditional families weren't always the strongest families. A single mother, who'd instilled in him morals and values and had taught him the importance of human dignity, had raised him. His half brothers had grown up with two parents, yet Brady and Seth were selfish, immature, back-stabbing jerks.

And you want to be a part of that family.

Lucas rubbed the back of his neck. Maybe he was a fool to believe that snagging a big client would earn him a place in the family, but he felt compelled to try. There were no guarantees that he and his father would develop the kind of relationship he'd dreamed of having since he'd been a kid, but if he didn't do his best, then he'd always wonder if he could have done more.

Lucas closed the door on thoughts of his family and studied Ava's apartment. It looked the same as the dress boutique downstairs—exposed brick walls and copper fixtures. Ava had added pops of color with red throw pillows and a red-and-white afghan folded across the back of a couch.

"Sorry that took so long," she said, after closing Sophie's door. "Her bedtime routine usually doesn't involve a visitor."

"I enjoyed reading to her. She's a keeper."

"I'm making myself a cup of hot chocolate. Would you like one?"

"Sure. I haven't had hot chocolate since I was a kid."

"Don't get too excited. It's instant." She opened the pantry door and took out packets of dry cocoa mix and a bag of mini marshmallows.

"I grew up on instant everything," he said.

"If you want to take a walk down memory lane—" she nodded to the shelves of food "—that's a kid-friendly pantry."

His gaze traveled over the items.

"Thankfully my mother-in-law cooks from scratch and Sophie eats several healthy meals a week at her house." Ava filled two mugs with water and put them in the microwave. A minute later she removed the mugs and dumped the packets of chocolate mix into the hot water then stirred.

"Thanks," he said, taking his mug.

She walked into the living room and he followed her, his eyes dropping to the gentle sway of her hips. She sat on the end of the couch and he took the middle cushion. He sipped his cocoa, wishing there wasn't five inches of space separating them. He wanted to run his fingers through her hair and discover for himself if the strands felt as soft as they appeared.

"You said why you were in town but you never said why you picked Marietta to hide out from your family." Ava's eyes twinkled above the rim of her mug. "There are warmer places to visit than Montana in January."

"I suppose it seems strange but it's not a coincidence that I came here." He set his hot chocolate on a drink coaster. "I was born here."

Her eyes widened. "Really?"

"My mom didn't like to talk about the past but she confessed that after she'd told my father she was pregnant with me, he gave her money to leave town."

"That's terrible."

Lucas thought so, too.

"What about your mother's parents?"

"They disowned her."

"That's so sad. I can't imagine ever not wanting Sophie in my life, no matter what kind of mistakes she makes."

"The bus money brought her as far as Marietta before it ran out. She ended up giving birth to me here and staying for two years before returning to San Diego."

"So you came back to see your old stomping grounds."

He nodded. "When I sorted through my mom's things I found a slew of handwritten notes that she'd saved from our time here."

"Like a diary?"

He nodded. "She'd made a list of people in town who'd been kind to us. She'd always hoped to return one day to thank them again."

"I've only been in Marietta a couple of years but I believe this town is special."

"I spent hours putting all of the notes into a document on my computer. When my father asked me to get lost for a while, I thought it would be the perfect opportunity to carry out my mother's wish." He finished his hot chocolate. "The problem is I lost the flash drive with all the information at the hotel Sunday night. It must have fallen out of my pocket during the New Year's Eve party."

The color drained from Ava's face, leaving her skin as white as the snow falling outside. "What's wrong?"

"Oh, no."

He reached for her hand, but she sprang off the couch. She went over to the door and shoved her feet into a pair of boots then slipped into her jacket and pulled on a pair of mittens.

"Where are you going?" he asked.

"To find something."

"Now?"

"I'll be right back." She left the apartment and Lucas went to the window and watched her descend the fire escape. When Ava reached the pavement, she slogged through the snow to the Dumpster.

No way. She wasn't going to…

Ava lifted the lid and pushed it behind the container then attempted to climb the side of the bin. When her foot slipped and she fell, landing on her rump, Lucas sprang into action. He threw on his coat and gloves and went after her.

"Ava!" he shouted into the wind when he reached the bottom of the stairs. She either didn't hear him or intended to ignore him because she made a second attempt to climb into the container. By the time he reached her, she was teetering over the edge, her fanny sticking up in the air. Lucas wrapped his arms around her legs, fearing she'd fall on her head.

"What are you doing?" she yelled.

"Keeping you—" *crazy beautiful woman* "—from falling."

"I have to find it."

"Find what?" he asked.

"Your flash drive."

My flash drive? "Why would the drive be in the Dumpster?"

She leaned farther over the edge, pressing her coat-covered fanny against his face. "I threw it away."

When the meaning of her words sunk in, he relaxed his hold and Ava fell forward, her boot clipping his chin. She tumbled headfirst into the Dumpster. "Ava!" He hoisted himself up and peered over the edge.

She lay sprawled across a mound of cardboard boxes, glaring at him.

"I'm sorry." He extended his arm. "Grab my hand."

She obeyed but instead of getting to her feet, she tugged hard and Lucas tumbled over the edge, almost landing on top of her.

"What did you do that for?" he asked, stunned that she'd tricked him.

She climbed to her knees and moved boxes aside. "You can help me look for it."

"Should I be concerned that you know your way around the inside of a Dumpster?"

"Ha. Ha. This is the first time I've crawled into one of these things and hopefully it will be the last."

"Actually it doesn't smell so bad," he said.

"I'm the only one who throws household garbage in it. It's mostly shipping boxes and packaging material from the dress shop." She pulled a white garbage bag out from beneath a box in the corner. "Here it is."

His gaze swung between the bag and Ava's face. "How did my flash drive end up in there?"

"I found a drive on the ballroom floor New Year's Eve and it didn't have the Big Sky Mavericks on it. I thought it was one of the prizes being given away and figured the printer had missed stamping it with the logo." She opened the bag and moved the snotty tissues. "Here it is." She handed Lucas the drive then closed the bag and knotted the ties again. She made a move to stand but he caught her arm.

"Wait." He stared into her eyes. "I really want to kiss you."

Chapter Six

AVA SUCKED IN a quick breath, the cold air crystalizing in her lungs as she lost herself in Lucas's blue eyes. Protected from the howling wind outside the Dumpster, thick snowflakes fell from the sky, sticking to his hair and dark lashes.

Sometimes alone in bed at night Ava yearned for the gentle touch of a man's hand gliding over her skin. The feel of beard stubble pricking her cheek. A hairy leg sliding between her calves. And instead of a soft pillow, a muscular chest to lay her weary head on. But never once had she fantasized about kissing a man inside a commercial trash bin.

His face drew closer and she released a soft sigh when his cold lips brushed hers. A tingling sensation spread through her chest, as he deepened the kiss, leaving her light-headed. Feeling as if she were tumbling, she clutched his jacket and hung on tight, giving herself over to the moment.

Lucas ended the kiss and then nuzzled her frozen cheek. "The snow is coming down harder. We should go inside."

She wished they could remain where there were a little longer, because once they returned to the apartment and she told him about the co-op, the intimacy of this moment would vanish. Lucas climbed out of the Dumpster first and then helped Ava to the ground. After he closed the lid, he took her hand and they slogged through the snow to the fire escape.

As they climbed the stairs, she asked, "Did you park your car on the street?"

"I walked over from the hotel."

At least four inches of snow covered the ground and there was no sign of the storm letting up. The longer he remained at her apartment the less likely it was that he'd be able to return to the hotel.

There's always the couch.

Of course he'd sleep on the sofa. Even though Sophie approved of Mr. Lucas, Ava would never want her daughter to find her mother in bed with a man she wasn't married to.

People will talk when they discover he stayed at your apartment.

Even so, she didn't have the heart to send Lucas back to the hotel during a snowstorm. He was more than just a businessman after Sandra's building—he was a man who made her daughter giggle. Who loved his mother and wanted to fulfill her last wishes. He was a man who yearned to be part of his newfound family. A man trying to make his father proud.

When they reached the landing, he brushed the snow off of her hair and asked, "What's wrong?"

"I was just thinking I could use another cup of hot chocolate."

"Sounds good." He opened the door then followed her inside. They removed their winter gear and then Ava checked on Sophie. The imp was sound asleep, her teddy bear tucked close. She returned to the kitchen and asked, "Are you hungry?"

"I've been eyeing that pie on the counter. Is it apple?"

She nodded. "I forgot I bought it this afternoon after I picked up Sophie from preschool." She fetched plates and forks and dished out two servings of pie.

"My mother only baked from scratch at Christmastime. She'd frost cookies while I decorated the tree." He glanced across the room. "Did you have a tree this year?"

Ava put two mugs filled with water in the microwave. "I took our tree down a few days after Christmas. I always worry it'll catch fire. I think next year Sophie and I will shop for an artificial tree like my mother-in-law's, so we can keep it up longer." Ava finished making the hot chocolate then they carried their desserts and drinks to the living room and sat on the couch.

"This is excellent," he said after taking a bite of the pie.

They ate in silence for a minute then he set his plate down and studied her. "You've been on edge since I arrived for dinner." He tucked a strand of hair behind her ear, his finger lingering against the skin on her neck. "What's bothering you?"

She drew in a steadying breath. "I have bad news."

He smiled. "You already have a boyfriend."

She wished it were that simple. "Lucas, there's more going on with Sandra's dress shop and this building than you know."

"What do you mean?"

"Before the judge told you he wanted Sandra to get rid of the business so they could travel, I had already scheduled a meeting with her this morning to discuss a business proposal."

"I'm not following."

"Sandra and I met before you arrived at her shop and she'd agreed to consider my proposal. She'd forgot you were stopping by."

"You've lost me, Ava." He leaned forward clasping his hands between his knees. "What kind of business plan are you referring to? Do you have another job besides the housekeeping position at the hotel?"

She popped off the couch and paced a few feet away. "I have a bachelor of arts in business." His eyes widened and she rushed on. "I've been going to school part-time for years and finally earned my degree last spring. The job at the hotel pays the bills but my passion is to start a co-op."

"Congratulations on earning the degree. It must have been difficult, studying, working and taking care of Sophie."

Ava appreciated Lucas's validation. The only people who'd celebrated with her after she'd received her diploma had been Tilly and Sophie. And neither of them had understood what a big deal Ava's achievement had been.

"I'd love to hear more about the co-op," he said.

"The business will support single mothers interested in furthering their education. The women donate their time to the co-op in return for financial assistance toward their education goals." She paused, waiting for his reaction.

"I'm intrigued," he said. "Tell me more."

The earnest expression in his eyes insisted his interest was sincere, which made sense since a single mother had raised him.

"The co-op will sell refurbished vintage furniture and décor. I've been looking for a place to open the store but the spaces available in Marietta are charging too much in rent."

"How many women are involved?"

"Right now ten. Our hope is to grow and expand into the surrounding rural communities. This morning I asked Sandra to considering letting us use the basement of the building as a workshop and then the back rooms for our store and daycare."

"What you're doing is commendable," he said. "My mother wished she'd had the chance to go to college. I know it bothered her that the ladies she worked with at the bank had degrees and she didn't."

Ava was relieved Lucas understood. "The members of the co-op are depending on me to make this happen. Marietta is a small town and we help our own but—" she offered a soft smile "—single mothers are notorious for being proud and they're willing to put in the hard work for a chance to better themselves."

"You said it's been tough to find a place you can afford to lease. Would Sandra give you a good deal on the rent?"

"If she agrees to my proposal, she wouldn't charge us any rent." His mouth went slack and she said, "In lieu of rent the women in the co-op would also work in the dress shop whenever Sandra and the judge traveled." She mulled over her final thought searching for the right words to soften the blow. "If Sandra accepts my proposal, Lucas, then there's no need for her to sell the building." When he didn't say anything she broke the silence.

"I'm sorry, Lucas. It's just crazy that we both set our sights on Sandra's property." She took her half-eaten slice of pie into the kitchen and dumped it in the garbage, her stomach too upset to eat more.

"Ava."

She jumped when Lucas's hands clasped her shoulders. He turned her around and stared into her eyes. "Don't worry. We'll figure something out. Everything will be fine."

There wasn't anything left to figure out—unless Sandra's lawyer objected to the co-op, she had first dibs on the building. Lucas tipped her chin. "I admire you for wanting to better the lives of single mothers. One day, Sophie's going to recognize what a strong, amazing role model you are." He checked his watch. "It's almost ten o'clock. I better leave."

He pulled her close and kissed her again. She could get used to Lucas's kisses: gentle, soft, coaxing. And they always ended too soon. When he released her, Ava walked across the room and opened the door. An icy blast of wind hit her in the face. The snow on the stoop was almost to Ava's knees and still falling hard. Stupid weather people—they never got the forecast right. Flurries my foot; it was a full-blown blizzard with whiteout conditions. She slammed the door closed. "You can't walk back to the hotel tonight."

"It's only a few blocks away," he said.

"Doesn't matter. You're from San Diego."

He chuckled. "What's that supposed to mean?"

"You'll freeze to death by the time you reach the end of the alley." Her gaze swung to the couch.

"What about Sophie?" he asked.

"I'll set my alarm and you can leave in the morning before she wakes up. I'm sure the snow will stop in a few hours and the plows are usually out early."

"Are you sure?"

In that moment with his blue eyes boring into her, Ava had never been more sure of anything in her life. "Have you ever watched the movie *It's a Wonderful Life* with Jimmy Stewart?"

"It was one of my mother's favorites."

"I usually watch it every winter." She hesitated before she put the movie into the DVD player. "That was thoughtless of me," she said. "Maybe you'd rather pick a different movie?"

He shook his head. "I'm in the mood for Jimmy Stewart." After she joined him on the couch, he said, "I watched movies with my mother after her chemo treatments. We'd binge-watch her favorites all weekend long."

Ava expelled a loud sigh. "I don't get it."

"What?"

"Why you're not married or at least in a serious relationship. You should hear the stories the women in the co-op tell about their ex-husbands and boyfriends and what jerks they are."

"I'm glad you don't think I'm a jerk."

"Far from it. You're almost perfect."

He grinned. "I have my faults."

She'd like to see one or two of them, because so far Lucas Kendrick was batting a thousand.

"I was in a serious relationship before my mother became ill," he said.

A sliver of jealousy pricked Ava, but she shoved it aside. She was curious about the woman who'd captured his heart. "What happened?"

"Jenny and I met at work and dated on and off for a year then exclusively for another year before we moved in together. We'd talked about marriage but we were both busy with our careers. We agreed to wait to get engaged until we were settled in our jobs."

It didn't sound like it was love at first sight—not that Ava believed in that nonsense.

"Two weeks after my mother received her cancer diagnosis, Jenny left."

"That's awful." The woman had left Lucas all alone to deal with his mom's uncertain future.

"Some people don't do death well and Jenny was one of them."

He was making excuses for her.

"I was angry and upset that she'd left me when I needed her most."

"I'm sorry it didn't work out, Lucas."

"I didn't realize it then but Jenny leaving me was a gift."

"A gift?"

He blinked hard. "I was able to spend all of my free time with my mother and I was there to help her through every step of her journey. I'll never regret that."

Ava's eyes stung with tears. She doubted she'd ever meet another man like Lucas. Stupid fate. Why did he have to be from out of town? And why did she have to meet him after she'd decided to put roots down in Marietta?

She leaned over and kissed his cheek then reached for the remote and started the movie. Lucas put his arm around her and spread the red-and-white striped afghan over their laps. Ava snuggled against his side and drifted off to sleep in minutes.

❯❯❯❯❮❮❮❮

LUCAS FELT A puff of cool air hit his cheek early Wednesday morning and the image of him and Ava strolling hand-in-hand along Mission Beach in San Diego faded from his mind. Something soft tickled the side of his neck and he opened one eye and saw his reflection in the wire-rimmed glasses inches from his nose.

Chocolate-scented breath fanned his face. "Are you dead, Mr. Lucas?"

Uh-oh. What happened to Ava setting her alarm and waking him before her daughter crawled out of bed? "Do I look dead?" he whispered.

The sprite sat on the edge of the coffee table. She wore the tiara he'd bought for her and held a spoon in one hand and a jar of Nutella in the other. After they'd watched the movie last night, Ava had brought him an extra pillow from her bed before saying good night and disappearing into her room.

He'd lain awake for a long time staring at the ceiling, trying to figure out how he was going to tell Stan Mueller that Sandra Reynolds's building might not be available. He'd finally fallen asleep after convincing himself not to worry until his scheduled call with the businessman the day after tomorrow. Hopefully by then Sandra would have made a decision about the property.

He rolled to a sitting position and rubbed a hand down his tired face. "Is that your breakfast?" He nodded to the jar.

Her head bobbed and a strand of her brown hair got stuck in the goo on the spoon. "Hold still." He pulled the sticky lock free and tucked it behind her ear.

"How come you're sleeping out here?" she asked.

"There was too much snow on the ground last night and I couldn't walk back to the hotel."

She set the jar and spoon down then raced to her room, pajama feet slapping against the floor. A moment later she returned and sat on the coffee table again. "It's not snowing anymore."

He eyed his coat hanging by the back door and rubbed his whiskers.

"Do those hurt?"

"Does what hurt?" he asked.

She touched his cheek with a sticky finger. "Those prickly things."

"Whiskers don't hurt." He nodded to the jar. "Aren't you supposed to put that stuff on a piece of bread?"

"Mommy puts it on my pancakes, but—" she looked over her shoulder at Ava's bedroom door then back at Lucas

"—she's sleeping."

"What if I make you pancakes?" He got up from the couch and went into the kitchen.

Sophie followed, standing near him as he perused the contents of the pantry. "I can help," she said.

"Okay." He set her on a stool at the island. "Don't move." He returned to the pantry, grabbed the box of pancake mix and set it on the counter. Then he wet a paper towel and wiped the chocolate off of Sophie's hair, chin and fingers. "Better?"

She smiled, her eyes as big as saucers behind the lenses of her glasses.

"Stick with me, kid—I know what I'm doing." He rummaged through the cupboards. "Where does your mom keep the mixing bowls?" Sophie pointed at a lower cabinet where he found plastic bowls in various sizes. He took out a measuring cup, measuring spoons and a whisk. "I think we're set."

He opened the powdered mix then set the measuring cup in front of her. "Fill it to the top."

Sophie tipped the box and mix spilled onto the back of Lucas's hand. "That's good." She set the box down. "Now dump the measuring cup into the bowl." He went to the fridge and took out two eggs. "Do you know how to crack an egg?"

She shook her head.

"Watch me, then you can try." He tapped the egg against the side of the bowl then opened the shell and dumped the yolk into the mix. "Your turn." He handed the second egg to her. Instead of tapping the egg Sophie smashed it against the bowl and the yolk hit the counter then slid onto the floor.

"Oops."

"Oops is right, kid." He fetched another egg and added it to the mix then measured a cup of water and Sophie poured the liquid into the bowl. "Stir slowly."

He wet more paper towels and bent down to wipe the egg off the floor under her chair. He'd almost finished when it began snowing flour. He glanced up and a glob of batter landed on the front of his shirt.

"Sophie, what are you doing?" Ava's voice rang out.

"Making pancakes with Mr. Lucas."

"Where's Mr. Lucas?"

"Mr. Lucas is right here." He stood.

Ava's eyes widened. "Oh, dear."

"Sophie got a little carried away stirring the batter." He soaked in the sight of Ava in the morning—soft and sleepy-eyed, hair snarled, no makeup. Touchable. Beautiful.

"Mr. Lucas said I could help, Mommy."

Ava's mouth twitched with an effort not to laugh. "How about I finish making the pancakes and Mr. Lucas can take a quick shower and rinse the flour out of his hair?" She went into the laundry room and returned with a clean bath towel. "Take off your shirt, and I'll wash it before the stain sets."

Lucas removed his dress shirt and noticed the batter had also stained his undershirt.

"Your T-shirt, too." Ava held out her hand.

He handed her the cotton garment and when she continued to stare at his chest, he glanced down at himself.

"What's the matter?"

"Nothing." She shoved the bath towel at him then retreated to the laundry room.

Lucas winked at Sophie and smiled all the way to the bathroom, thinking his three-day-a-week workouts at the fitness center were paying off. He hopped into the shower and stood beneath the hot spray, shampooing his hair with floral-smelling soap. He thought about the two brown-eyed, brown-haired beauties in the other room and for a man who wasn't a fan of cold weather, he decided he could grow fond of blizzards if it meant hiding somewhere with Ava to wait the storm out.

The past few years Lucas had been living in the moment, taking care of his mother and then after her death focusing day-to-day on establishing a relationship with his father. Meeting Ava and Sophie reminded him that he still wanted to get married and have kids—he didn't care to end up alone like his mother.

He shook his head sending suds flying against the wall. This place—Marietta—was messing with his brain. Even though he'd been born here, he had no memory of the town yet everywhere he went and everyone he spoke with felt oddly familiar, but feeling nostalgic didn't explain his growing attraction to Ava and the need to protect her and Sophie. Marietta was a far cry from San Diego with few to no job opportunities for a man in his line of work. Besides, he'd just connected with his father. If he left San Diego now they'd never grow close.

He rinsed his hair then turned off the water. Instead of

thinking up excuses to kiss Ava he should devise another plan to win Stan Mueller's business, if Sandra refused to sell. Ava had surprised him last night when she'd revealed she had a college degree like him. He'd admired her strength and determination. Unlike his mother who'd taken what life had dished out, Ava had gone after what she wanted.

He had no intention of getting in the way of Ava's co-op, but he was worried that if he didn't find a property for Mueller, he'd have to wait for another opportunity to show his father and half brothers that he was fully invested in the family business. Later today he'd contact a local Realtor and ask about other historical buildings for sale in the area.

When he stepped from the tub, he spotted a T-shirt on the counter. Ava must have left it for him to wear while his clothes were in the laundry. After drying off he pulled on his jockey shorts and pants then unfolded the gray shirt and chuckled at the image of a pink kitten. He checked the tag—XL. He tugged it on, the material stretching over his chest like shrink-wrap.

"Is breakfast ready?" He stopped in front of Sophie. She pointed at the kitten on his shirt and giggled.

"Are you making fun of my clothes?" He faked outrage and Ava laughed.

"I won that as a door prize at a birthday party. It's the largest T-shirt I own."

"For future reference, I like dogs better." He sat on the stool by Sophie, and Ava set a plate of pancakes in front of him then moved the butter dish and syrup closer. "Would you like a glass of milk?"

"Sure, thanks."

"I want a dog, but Mommy says we can't have one 'cause we don't have a yard." Sophie looked at her mother. "How come our dog can't live at Nana's house?"

"Because Nana would forget to take the dog outside." Ava turned on the radio. "How about a little music with breakfast?"

Lucas smiled at Ava's attempt to change the conversation. His mother had never let him have a pet, either—mostly because of the cost. Lucas had settled for playing with his friends' animals.

"That was "Dime Store Cowgirl" by Kacey Musgraves and you're listening to KCMC country radio. Back in thirty seconds with news and weather."

Ava poured more batter onto the griddle and Sophie chatted about wanting a girl dog. Lucas listened with half an ear, his gaze straying to Ava. Her pink fuzzy bathrobe was large enough for two. He imagined opening the front and joining her inside the warm coat, his chest pressing against hers, their heartbeats thumping to the same rhythm.

"It's the top of the hour at KCMC. Dylan Morgan here with breaking news. David Reyes, manager of the Graff Hotel, has filed a missing person's report on one of the guests."

Ava's eyes rounded.

"San Diego resident Lucas Kendrick did not return to the hotel after departing on foot yesterday around six p.m. It's possible the Californian may have become disoriented in the snowstorm. If anyone has seen Mr. Kendrick or knows of his whereabouts please call the sheriff's department or contact Mr. Reyes at the hotel."

Lucas pointed his fork at the radio. "That was a joke, right?"

Ava shook her head. "Several years ago a guest had car trouble outside of town and attempted to walk to the hotel on foot in a snowstorm." Ava rubbed her brow. "I forgot that the staff keeps close track of who comes and goes. I should have had you phone the front desk last night to tell them that you wouldn't be returning."

"That's taking small-town hospitality to new lengths." He stuffed another forkful of pancake into his mouth and chewed. "As soon as I finish eating, I'll check in with the hotel."

Ava's eyes darted to Sophie. "What are you going to tell them?"

"That I'm okay. Do I have to tell them any more than that?"

"No."

He swallowed the last bite on his plate then pulled out his cell and spoke to Siri. "The Graff Hotel, Marietta, Montana." A few seconds later the number connected and he said, "This is Lucas Kendrick, I'm—" He waited for Bob to express his relief at hearing his voice.

"Yes, I know I didn't return to the hotel last night." He glanced at Ava. "Where am I?"

Her eyes widened.

"No need to worry, I'm fine. I'll be returning to the hotel later this morning. Thank you." He disconnected the call.

"I'm full," Sophie said.

"Brush your teeth." Ava cleared her plate away.

When Sophie disappeared into the bathroom, Lucas walked over to Ava and grasped her arms. "I won't tell anyone where I spent the night."

"Thank you."

He didn't have much time before the pip-squeak returned and he really wanted to kiss Ava. He brushed his mouth lightly over hers. "When can I see you again?"

"I'm done!" Sophie raced past the kitchen and ran into her bedroom.

Ava took the dishrag and wiped down the countertop. "You'd better get going."

"My shirt isn't dry," he reminded her.

She peeked at him then looked away. "I'll drop it off at the front desk when I go into work on Thursday."

"Mr. Lucas!" Sophie skidded to a halt in front of him and pushed her glasses up her nose.

Amused, Lucas said, "Yes, Princess Sophie?"

"Will you take me ice-skating?"

"I told you we're going this Saturday," Ava said.

"Can Mr. Lucas come with us?"

He joined Sophie in sending Ava a hopeful look.

"Fine." Ava laughed. "Mr. Lucas can go, too."

"I'll pick you ladies up at one o'clock."

"Can Nana come?" Sophie asked him.

Lucas would rather not have a chaperone. "The more the merrier."

"Yay!" Sophie hugged his leg, knocking him off balance.

He caught himself on the edge of the island. "Whoa there, princess."

She released his leg then returned to her bedroom.

"Plan on stopping at the chocolate shop after skating. I've been told I can't leave town until I try their hot cocoa."

"Sage's special recipe is to die for," she said.

He pulled out his phone and looked at her. "I should put your number in my contacts."

"Sure." She rattled off the digits.

Lucas went to the door and shrugged into his parka, then laced up his boots before tugging on his cap and gloves.

"Be careful on the steps," she said.

"Where's your shovel? I'll clear the snow off before I leave."

"Thanks for offering, but Sandra pays a local high school boy to shovel. He'll be here before noon."

"What about your mother-in-law? Why don't I stop by her house and shovel before I head to the hotel."

"I'd planned to help her this afternoon."

"Tell me where she lives and I'll take care of it." He smiled. "Payment for breakfast."

"You don't have—"

"I want to."

She wrote down the address and handed him the slip of paper. "It's one block over from the Sunset Apartments."

"I know where the apartments are." He stuffed the note into his jean pocket then pointed at the magnet to-do pad stuck to the fridge door. "Item three on the list is my cell number."

"Mr. Lucas!" Sophie came flying out of her bedroom, waving a pink piece of construction paper. She skidded to a stop in front of him and held out the paper. "Do you like it?"

Lucas spent a few seconds looking at the sketch. "Is that a castle house?"

Sophie nodded. "And that's you." She pointed at the stick figure and his chest constricted.

"Is that a crown on my head?"

"Yes, 'cause you're a prince."

He noticed his smile was wider than his face and that he held the hand of a much smaller stick figure with glasses and long hair. "Can I keep this, Sophie?"

She nodded. "Bye, Mr. Lucas." She ran back to her room.

Lucas folded the paper and slipped it into his coat pocket. He sent Ava a smile then left, closing the door tightly behind him. He drew in several deep breaths of cold air before descending the steps. The pint-sized princess was weaving a magical spell on Lucas. As he trudged through the snow he acknowledged the enormous responsibility Ava carried on her shoulders to protect Sophie's feelings. Lucas's mom had never dated—at least not anyone he could remember—so she'd never had to worry about him growing attached to a man who might abandon them down the road.

He knew Sophie liked him but not until he'd seen her drawing had he considered the consequences of whatever he and Ava were doing with each other.

Maybe by the time he reached the mother-in-law's house he'd figure out what to call his and Ava's relationship.

Chapter Seven

"TILLY, IT'S AVA."

"Hello, dear."

"I'm checking in after the snowstorm last night." Ava wanted to give her mother-in-law advance warning that Lucas was headed her way.

"I'm fine, dear. The plows have already been down the street."

"Lucas Kendrick is coming by to shovel your walk."

"The man who calls Sophie princess?"

Ava nodded then realized her mother-in-law couldn't see her. "Were you listening to the radio this morning?"

"No, why?"

"Lucas was reported missing but he wasn't really missing." Ava would rather Tilly hear this from her than second-hand from a neighbor. "Lucas stopped by the apartment last night to ask questions about Sandra's business and I wasn't paying attention to the weather. When he was ready to leave there was too much snow on the ground to walk back to the hotel and..." She sounded like a blithering idiot. "He slept on the couch." She waited for Tilly's reaction.

"Why is he shoveling my walk?"

The air escaped Ava's lungs in an audible whoosh.

"When I told him I planned to help you shovel later today, he volunteered."

"I'll put on a pot of coffee."

"I don't think he intends to stay long."

"Shoveling is hard work," she said. "I made a fresh batch of homemade chicken soup yesterday. I'll heat that up for him."

Ava felt a headache coming on and pressed her fingertips to her temple. "Before I forget to tell you, Lucas offered to take Sophie and me ice-skating on Saturday and he invited you to come with us." *Please say you don't want to go.*

"How nice. I think my skates are in the basement some-where. I'll look for them later today."

Great. "If you need anything let me know, otherwise I'll see you tomorrow when I pick up Sophie." The preschool van dropped Sophie off at Tilly's in the afternoon on Tuesdays and Thursdays when Ava worked.

"That's fine, dear. See you then."

Ava disconnected the call and stared at the piece of paper with Lucas's number. She shouldn't enter it in her phone, because nothing long-term was going to happen between them. His life was in San Diego and hers was in Marietta.

"Mommy?" Sophie walked into the kitchen and climbed onto a stool.

"What, honey?"

"Can we make cookies?"

Ava had just finished cleaning up after Sophie and Lucas's pancake-making disaster. "Sure." Baking would take her mind off Lucas and the empty feeling in her apartment now that he was gone.

"I wanna make a cookie for Mr. Lucas 'cause he's gonna take us ice-skating."

Apparently Sophie was determined that their overnight guest stayed on their minds all day. Her daughter's infatuation with Lucas was sweet and concerning. Ava worried not only about her feelings but her little girl's heart, too; because once Lucas accomplished what he'd come to Marietta to do, he'd return to sunny San Diego and leave Ava and Sophie behind in the cold.

>>>><<<<

LUCAS MADE IT as far as the train depot on Front Avenue before the sound of a siren reached his ears. A patrol car pulled alongside him and the policeman lowered the passenger-side window.

"Officer." Lucas walked over to the vehicle.

"You wouldn't happen to be Lucas Kendrick?"

"That would be me."

"I'm patrolman Scott Bliven. Are you aware you've been reported missing?"

"Yes, sir. I checked in with the Graff Hotel a short while ago."

The officer reached for his radio. "Betty. This is Scott. I found our missing person."

A squeaky voice came through the speaker. "Copy. Dead or alive?"

Lucas grinned.

"Alive. Cancel the search."

"Copy that. Scott?"

"What?"

"Mable Bramble called again."

"What now?"

"Bill Kennedy took out another bush when he plowed the driveway at the bed and breakfast."

"Tell her what we always tell her," Bliven said.

"Copy that."

"What do you usually tell Ms. Bramble?" Lucas asked.

"If she'd like to shovel her own driveway, she's more than welcome to." Bliven nodded to the car door. "I'll give you a lift to the hotel."

"Actually I'm on my way to First Avenue to shovel Mrs. Moore's sidewalk."

"Hop in." He pointed to the trash and folders on the passenger seat and said, "You'll have to sit in the back."

Lucas got in and fastened his seat belt. "This is the first time I've ridden in a patrol car." He made eye contact with the cop in the rearview mirror. "I'd planned to stop by the police station before I left town."

"Oh?"

"I'm looking for information on a patrolman who helped my mother years ago."

"What's your mother's name?"

"Carol Kendrick. She lived in Marietta in the late eighties."

"Who's the officer?" Bliven asked.

"Henry Stubben."

"Henry retired years ago. He and his wife live in Florida."

"That's too bad. He bought my mother a meal when she was down on her luck."

"Sounds like Henry." Bliven parked in front of the turquoise house Lucas had stopped at when he'd first arrived in town. "This is Mrs. Moore's home?"

The front door opened and the same whacky redheaded woman he'd spoken with Sunday afternoon stepped onto the porch and waved. She was Ava's mother-in-law?

"Thank you for the lift." Lucas got out of the car and the policeman drove away.

"Hello, Lucas. Ava said you were coming by."

"Mrs. Moore." He trudged up the snow-covered walk and climbed the porch steps. "I didn't realize you were related to Ava and Sophie."

"Call me Tilly." She handed him a shovel. "I've got chicken soup warming on the stove. When you finish come inside and eat." She shut the door in his face.

Lucas shoveled the steps first then tackled the sidewalk, tossing the snow on top of the menagerie of wildlife statues. By the time he'd cleared the walks, he'd worked up a thirst and an appetite. He returned the shovel to the porch and the front door opened before he had a chance to knock.

"Could I bother you for a glass of water?" he asked.

"Of course. Come inside."

He stepped on the rug in the entryway and stomped the snow off of his boots. The smell of baking bread reached his nose and his stomach growled.

"I need to take the rolls out of the oven."

While Tilly made noise in the kitchen, Lucas glanced around the living room, counting seven cuckoo clocks on the walls. A minute later Tilly returned with his drink. When he reached for the glass a cool breeze passed over his hand and he turned to see if he'd left the front door ajar. He hadn't.

He stared at the red liquid in the glass. Maybe she hadn't heard him ask for water. "What's this?"

"Kool-Aid."

He took a sip and smiled. "Fruit punch. My mom made this for me all the time when I was a kid."

"I know." Then she said, "All mothers make their kids Kool-Aid."

The clocks in the room struck eleven and for that many seconds he listened to a cacophony of squawking. After the birds retreated into their houses, he said, "That's a noisy bunch."

"What?" Tilly glanced to her side.

"I said that's a noisy—"

"I heard you."

Lucas wondered if Ava was aware of her mother-in-law's odd behavior. He finished the drink then held out the glass. "As soon as my toes warm up, I'll shovel the driveway."

"No need. I don't drive anymore. I let the neighborhood kids use my driveway to build snow forts." She nodded. "Hand me your coat."

When he shrugged out of his jacket her eyes widened and he glanced at himself then swallowed a groan. He'd forgotten he was wearing Ava's kitten T-shirt. "I can explain."

She glanced to her right. "I'd like to hear this explanation."

Lucas winced unsure how to describe what had transpired between him and Ava last night—not as much as he wished but more than he'd hoped. "I needed to speak with Ava about Sandra Reynolds's business. She invited me over for dinner and—"

"Ava cooked for you?"

Oh, boy. Maybe he shouldn't have mentioned that. "When it was time to leave, the snow was coming down pretty hard and the winds had picked up. Since I'd walked over to her apartment from the hotel Ava was generous enough to allow me sleep on her couch."

"That explains why you spent the night in her apartment but not why you're wearing her T-shirt."

He detected a glint of humor in Tilly's eyes and suspected the older woman enjoyed watching him squirm. "Sophie and I made pancakes for breakfast," he said, "and she spilled batter on my clothes. Ava threw my shirt into the washing machine and loaned me one of hers."

"Come into the kitchen."

Grateful she appeared satisfied with his explanation, he followed her to the back of the house. "Sure smells good in here, Mrs. Moore."

"Call me Tilly. And sit down. My kitchen isn't big and you're taking up all the space."

He pulled out a chair at the table near the window overlooking the yard. "How long have you lived in Marietta, Tilly?"

"Around thirty years," she said. "I grew up in Livingston, but a few months after Ralph and I married he got a job working as a fish and game warden and we moved here."

"Ava told me about your son. I'm sorry. He was too young to die."

"Thank you. Drew was a lot like his father. Always pushing the envelope. Ralph died on the job, trying to rescue a man who was ice fishing in the mountains. The ice broke under his weight and they both drowned."

"That's awful," he said. "I'm sorry." The older woman had experienced her share of grief.

"Both of them died doing what they loved. I take comfort in that." She placed a bowl of steaming soup in front of Lucas then dished out a smaller bowl for herself.

"This is a real treat. Thank you."

"You're welcome." She retrieved a basket of warm rolls and set them on the table and then sat across from him.

"You're pulling out all the stops."

"My granddaughter says you call her Princess Sophie."

He chuckled. "Cinderella's her favorite bedtime story." He shoveled a spoonful of soup into his mouth. "This is excellent."

"It's been a long time since I've had a man eat at my table."

"Your kitchen reminds me of the times I stopped by my mother's apartment after work. She had a small TV on the counter and we'd watch *Seinfeld* reruns and eat microwavable dinners."

After Lucas worked his way up the career ladder, he'd

given his mother extra money to spend on groceries, but she was happiest eating two-dollar frozen meals. "Carol misses you."

The spoon froze halfway to his mouth. Had he told Tilly his mother's name? He couldn't remember.

"Chicken soup is good for the soul," she said, "not just the stomach."

"That's exactly what my mother used to say."

"Mothers say a lot of smart things."

Lucas finished his meal. He hadn't felt this mellow in a long time and he blamed it on the homemade soup, spending time with Ava and Sophie and his workout shoveling snow. He could get used to more days like this.

"What brought you to Marietta in January?" she asked.

"A couple of things, but I blame a spat with my father's wife for visiting in the middle of the winter."

Tilly's eyebrows climbed up her forehead.

"I just recently connected with my biological father and his wife and sons believe I have an ulterior motive for coming forward."

"Do you?"

He shook his head. "My father wasn't involved in my life when I was growing up and I promised my mother before she passed away that I'd reach out to him."

"Ava says I can be a little nosy sometimes but since she's not here—" Tilly winked "—I can pry. How are things going with your father?"

"After we met he offered me a job at his company." Lucas reached for a second roll. "Growing up I'd convinced myself that I didn't need a father but it's been nice having him recognize my hard work." He paused to butter the roll. "In the short time since we connected, he's taught me a lot about the business."

"I sense a but in there somewhere."

"But no matter how hard I work, Claire and my half brothers aren't cutting me any slack."

"If your father's not worried, then you shouldn't be, either."

"I try to ignore her but she's intent on sabotaging my relationship with my dad."

"How's that?"

"The few times he's invited me to lunch or dinner Claire had some kind of emergency." Lucas had been deeply disappointed that Roger hadn't seen what his wife was trying to do.

"What about your brothers?" Tilly asked.

"They're lazy." And jealous of the good work Lucas was doing on behalf of the company. In the beginning he had cut his brothers some slack because he didn't know how he'd feel if his father's long-lost offspring suddenly appeared out of the blue. Seth and Brady weren't responsible for the way things had worked out between Lucas's mom and their father, but Lucas would have thought they'd work harder at their jobs if they felt threatened. Instead of acting like adults, they bellyached like juveniles.

"Maybe you should move away from San Diego."

"San Diego's been home since I was two years old." Although Tilly's kitchen on a cold January day felt more welcoming than his California condo. He lifted his empty drinking glass. "May I?"

"Help yourself. The pitcher is in the fridge."

"You mentioned a couple of things brought you to Marietta," she said.

"I was born here." When sat down again, he said, "My mother stayed two years then returned to San Diego but she'd always wanted to come back and thank the people who'd helped us." He buttered a third roll. "First on her list to thank was Mable Bramble."

"The town matriarch is a curmudgeon." Tilly pursed her lips.

"Mable's a tough old bird, but she felt sorry for my mom." The dowager claimed she'd been more concerned with keeping the riffraff off of Marietta's streets, but Lucas genuinely believed she cared about the residents in this town more than she wanted to let on.

He set his spoon against the side of the empty bowl. "That hit the spot, thank you."

"Who else helped your mother?" Tilly asked.

"A policeman named Henry Stubben, but the officer who dropped me off at your house said Henry retired to Florida."

"Well, your mother appreciates your efforts."

Tilly was an odd duck, talking about Lucas's mom in the present tense. He shoved his chair back and carried his dishes to the sink. "Thank you again for the meal." He smiled. "And the conversation."

She followed him to the front door and watched him

stuff his feet into his boots and tie the laces. "I'm looking forward to ice-skating on Saturday."

"Me, too," he said.

Tilly opened the door. "Thank you for shoveling."

He stepped onto the porch and put on his hat and gloves.

"Of course I think he's nice."

Lucas turned. "Pardon?"

"I said have a nice day." The door closed.

When Lucas arrived at the hotel, Ron was there to greet him at the door.

"Mr. Kendrick, we were worried about you when you didn't return last night."

"I appreciate the concern but I was fine."

"Glad to hear, sir." He nodded to the chairs across the lobby. "Officer Bliven would like a word with you."

"Thanks." Lucas walked over and shook the policeman's hand. "Scott."

"When I heard you'd left Mrs. Moore's, I headed over here."

Not even a blizzard slowed down the Marietta gossip-mongers. "What can I do for you?"

"After I dropped you off at Mrs. Moore's, I returned to the station and searched through the old log books to see what I could find out about the calls Henry Stubben took in the late eighties."

Talk about going above and beyond. "That's incredibly generous of you."

Bliven waved off Lucas's gratitude. "It's been a slow

week."

"Did you find anything?"

"Henry responded to a 911 call that came in on November fourth 1987 that might have involved your mother."

"What kind of call?"

"A resident on Railway Avenue, the street behind the hotel, reported seeing someone hanging around the Graff."

Lucas recalled his conversation with the judge at the ball. "I thought the hotel was boarded up back then."

"There was a chain-link fence around the lot." Bliven's gaze moved through the lobby before returning to Lucas. "How much do you know about the hotel's history?"

"Judge Kingsley mentioned the place had once been scheduled for demolition."

"The hotel opened in 1886 but a fire in 1912 destroyed it. A couple of years later it reopened and business was good until the stock market crash in 1929. After that the place struggled to survive. By the mid-seventies only the ballroom and restaurant were used for special events. Eventually like the judge told you, the building was slated for demolition until Troy Sheenan rescued it."

Lucas appreciated the history lesson but he was more interested in the 1987 November call. "Did Henry checked the hotel that night in November?"

"He did a drive-by and noticed a light coming from a basement windows. He walked the perimeter of the property, and when he circled back, the light was gone." Bliven raised his hands in the air. "A lot of people believe old buildings are haunted."

"You're saying a ghost was playing with the lights that night?"

"The electricity had been cut off to the building for a long time. It was either a ghost or someone with a flashlight or candle was squatting in the basement."

"Where does my mother fit into this story?"

"Henry went back to the hotel the following morning and found a hole in the fence. He checked the building but it was locked up tight, except for one window."

"The basement window where the light had been?"

Bliven nodded. "It had been propped open. Henry wrote in the report that he saw trash scattered on the floor. He assumed a vagrant or runaway was hiding down there."

"What did he do then?"

"He bought a meal from the diner and dropped it through the hotel window. I'm sure he was trying to be friendly so whoever was down there would come out and talk to him."

"Did they?"

"Nope."

Lucas had come across a business card in his mother's things. The edges had been bent and the printing had faded, but Officer's Stubben's name had still been legible.

"Henry returned to the hotel later that night and shined his light inside the window. The trash was gone so he figured the person had moved on."

Lucas had a difficult time imagining his mother hiding in the basement of an abandoned hotel, but maybe she'd sought shelter from the cold. Then again just because he'd found Henry's business card in his mother's possessions didn't mean she'd been the person in the hotel that night. The officer could have given his card to Lucas's mom during one of her shifts at the diner.

"I don't know if this information helps, but after you said your mother wanted to thank Henry..." Bliven shrugged.

"I appreciate what you did." Lucas shook the man's hand then rode the elevator to his room. If his mother had been staying in the basement and Henry had scared her off, it might explain why Mable had found her sitting at the bus stop in the cold that first week of November.

As soon as Lucas entered his room, he kicked off his boots and hung up his coat then opened his laptop and checked email. Nothing from his father or Stan Mueller, which meant he had time to speak with a Realtor before his Friday call with Stan.

He Googled real estate agencies and found Styles Realty Company on Main Street. An office assistant named Alisa set up an appointment with Tod Styles for later in the afternoon. Until then he'd grab a nap and dream about a brown-eyed princess—the older one.

Chapter Eight

FRIDAY AFTERNOON LUCAS parked the rental car on the street in front of the diner. Earlier that day Mable Bramble had left him a message at the front desk, informing him that Virginia Pritchard and her husband planned to stop in at the Main Street Diner around three o'clock.

Lucas was still processing what he'd learned about his mother on Wednesday from Officer Bliven and he was nervous about meeting his mother's former employer. The first person he'd reached out to for moral support had been Ava. She worked until three but had promised to stop by the diner after her shift ended.

When Lucas entered the restaurant, a short woman with dark hair and flashing dark eyes glanced up from behind the lunch counter.

"Welcome to the Main Street Diner, I'm Gabriella Marcos, the owner."

"Just the person I'm looking for." Lucas slid onto a swiveling stool covered in sparkly red leather. A radio by the cash register near the end of the counter played country music.

Her dark eyes assessed him and he had a feeling nothing escaped her notice. "You're not from around here." She set a white ceramic mug on the counter then fetched the coffee pot from the warmer. "And you take your Java black."

He chuckled. "Lucas Kendrick."

Her eyebrows arched. "Our missing person from Tuesday's snowstorm."

"I was never missing."

"Either way I'm glad you're okay." She winked. "We don't like to lose tourists."

Lucas glanced around, surprised the place was empty.

"There's usually a lull between the lunch and supper crowd." She checked over her shoulder. "My cook is taking a break, but I've got a pot of my famous Tex-Mex chili warming on the stove and fresh jalapeno cornbread."

"I had lunch earlier but I might have room for a small bowl."

"Coming right up." She disappeared into the kitchen.

The place was typical of those he'd eaten at in California. A brick wall separated the diner from the business next door. Booths sat in front of the windows and tables occupied the open area. The original wood flooring had been restored, giving the place a homey feel. A pass-through window behind the counter let customers watch the cook.

"It's the top of the hour and I'm Dylan Morgan with your KCMC weather update. Current temperature is twenty-six degrees. Saturday will be partly cloudy with a high of twenty-eight. Chance of flurries on Monday. Your weather report is brought to you by Don Steele Construction." Construction sounds came across the airwaves then faded. "We have an update on our missing person."

Gabriella delivered his chili with a teasing smile.

"We reported Graff Hotel guest Mr. Kendrick had been located Wednesday morning by Officer Scott Bliven on Railway Avenue. Mr. Kendrick was actually found wandering along First Avenue. Apologies for the misinformation."

"Wandering?" Gabriella asked.

"I was on my way to Tilly Moore's house to shovel her walk." He ducked his head and sampled a spoonful of chili. "Mmm." Not too spicy—just enough kick to make the taste buds beg for more. "What kind of meat is in this?" It wasn't hamburger.

"Sirloin."

"This is fantastic."

"Glad you like it."

She reached for a cleaning rag beneath the counter then wiped down a tray of sugar shakers.

"Ms. Marcos—"

"Gabriella, please."

"Gabriella. I'm hoping to run into Virginia or Herb Pritchard. Have they been by the diner?"

The owner shook her head. "Not yet. Who told you they were coming?"

"Mable Bramble. She said the couple owned the business in the late eighties."

"They did."

"My mother lived in Marietta back then and Virginia gave her a job waitressing."

Bells jingled and Gabriella smiled. "Here's Virginia now."

Lucas spun on his stool and watched the elderly couple

enter the business.

"Virginia, Herb," Gabriella said. "Come sit at the counter and I'll introduce you to this gentleman who's been waiting to meet you."

Virginia shrugged out of her coat and handed it to her husband, who tossed their jackets over the back of a booth.

"You must be Lucas Kendrick." Virginia sat down. "Mable said you were asking about me."

Gabriella poured a mug of coffee and set it in front of Virginia then spoke to Herb. "How would you like to help me make a few loaves of honey-wheat bread for the dinner crowd?" Virginia's husband skirted the counter and followed Gabriella into the kitchen.

"Herb got a bread machine for Christmas and Gabriella's been sharing recipes with him while we're in town." Virginia sipped her coffee. "Mable said you're Carol's son."

"I heard she talked you into hiring my mother as a waitress back in 1987."

Virginia's gaze roamed over Lucas. "You're Carol's boy, all right. Same blue eyes."

The diner door opened and Ava walked in. Her hair was pinned to the top of her head in a messy pile, loose tendrils cascading around her face. She looked innocent and sexy at the same time. He stood as she approached the counter, wanting to hug her for showing up.

"Ava, this is Virginia Pritchard," he said. "Virginia, Ava Moore. Ava works at the Graff."

The older woman nodded. "Nice to meet you."

Lucas motioned for Ava to take his seat then he slid onto

another stool. Gabriella emerged from the kitchen, filled a mug with coffee and set it in front of Ava. "I guess you've already met Lucas."

Ava nodded. "At the New Year's Eve ball Sunday night."

Gabriella pointed to Lucas's half-eaten chili then asked, "Can I get you something to eat?"

"I'm fine, thanks," Ava said.

"My mother worked for Virginia when we lived here," Lucas told Ava.

"I can't tell you how many times Carol has crossed my mind through the years." Virginia smiled. "I wondered what had happened to her after she left town with you."

"Mom returned to San Diego," he said.

"Mable told me Carol passed away. I'm sorry, Lucas."

"Thank you," he said. "I'm glad we could meet. I want to pass along my mother's thanks for giving her a job and helping to look out for me."

Virginia's eyes watered. "Carol was a hard worker. She never complained."

That sounded like his mom—strong and determined, just like the pretty, single mom sitting by him right now.

"Did your mother ever tell you that I let her bring you to the diner when she worked?"

Lucas shook his head.

"Henry brought an old crib down from our attic and you slept in the supply room off of the kitchen." She smiled. "Our customers called you *little man*. They took turns passing you around when you put up a fuss."

Lucas's throat grew tight and his eyes watered when he

envisioned strangers bouncing him on their knee while his mom took orders and delivered food to tables. He thought he might embarrass himself then Ava squeezed his knee, offering comfort, and he reined in his emotions.

Virginia sipped her coffee. "Carol wouldn't say who your daddy was."

"Roger Belfour. I work for his company now."

"I guess that's nice that you have a relationship with him." Virginia didn't sound impressed and who could blame her when she'd witnessed Lucas's mother struggle to make ends meet and care for a baby all by herself?

"What I don't understand," the older woman said, "is why Carol didn't give her two weeks' notice before she left town."

"Mom said Marietta was beginning to feel like home and the people here like her family." Lucas glanced at Ava. If *home* and *family* were a color, they'd be chestnut-brown like Ava's eyes. "Mom said if she didn't leave Marietta when she did she might never have had the courage to go."

"I still remember that day," Virginia said. "Carol was never late for her shift and when she didn't show up, I called Mable because your mother didn't have a phone in her apartment. Mable called the library." The older woman smiled. "Your mother spent a lot of her free time at the library reading to you. Anyway Carol hadn't come into the library that day." Virginia sighed. "Mable drove to her apartment and found a note on the door that said she was going home. If we'd known where home was I would have checked up on the two of you."

"My mother thought enough time had passed that her parents would welcome us back, but they didn't."

"I'm real sorry to hear that." Virginia offered a sad smile. "But Carol did just fine raising you on her own."

Lucas's mom had kept a roof over his head and his belly full while being both a mother and father to him. They hadn't had many possessions but his mom had pushed him in school and encouraged him to attend college. And he'd been fortunate that he'd received a scholarship, which had paid for his undergraduate degree.

"You mentioned working for your father. Is he married?" Virginia asked.

"Married with two sons," Lucas said.

"How do you like your new family?"

Family. That was not the word that came to mind when he pictured Claire, Brady and Seth. "We're still getting to know one another, but my father's not what I expected."

"Oh?"

Lucas shrugged. "I'm giving him a chance."

"I hope things work out for the two of you." She glanced at the pass-through window. "I better check on Herb before he breaks one of Gabriella's fancy appliances."

Lucas gave the older woman a hug. "Thank you for treating my mother kindly."

"Don't be a stranger around these parts. You were born here. Marietta will always be home no matter where you live." Virginia looked at Ava. "It was nice meeting you, dear."

"Likewise," Ava said.

After Virginia took her coffee mug and disappeared through the door behind the counter, Lucas nodded to a booth and he and Ava moved seats. "How much time do you have?" he asked.

She checked her phone. "I've got a few minutes before I pick Sophie up from her grandmother's."

He hadn't seen Ava since Wednesday. He thought he might run into her at the hotel but he hadn't. "How was work?"

"The same as every other day." She reached across the table and squeezed his hand. "Your mother sounded like an amazing woman."

He nodded.

"She touched a lot of lives in Marietta, Lucas."

"Speaking of mothers," he said, "I forgot to tell you that when I first arrived in in town, I saw your mother-in-law clearing the snow off of the decorations in her yard and I stopped to ask her for directions to the hotel."

Ava smiled. "It was such a treat for her to eat lunch with you the other day. I hope she didn't tease you about wearing my kitten T-shirt. I made sure she knew you'd slept on the couch."

The word *couch* brought to mind the drawing Sophie had made him—a sobering reminder that his and Ava's relationship didn't just concern them. There was another little person that had a stake in the game.

"Has the lawyer gotten back to Sandra on your proposal?" he asked.

"I spoke with her this morning and she's meeting with

him in a week."

"Stan wanted to fly up here on Monday to see the building, but I told him to hold off."

"Is he aware that Sandra is considering my co-op proposal?"

"He knows there's another interested party but I didn't share any details about your co-op with him." He glanced at the clock on the wall. "Before you have to leave," he said, "I wanted to mention that I met with a Realtor named Tod Styles."

"I know who he is."

"Tod says Sandra could get a million two or a million three for the building." That was a drop in the bucket for a guy like Mueller.

"I told Stan I had a Realtor searching for other properties in the area, but he's determined to get his hands on Sandra's building."

"I don't understand. Why are you trying to discourage your client?"

"Marietta is your home. I'm just a visitor." He rushed on. "The women you're trying to help need the co-op. I was hoping if I got Stan interested in a different property, Sandra would be forced to accept your proposal."

"I appreciate you thinking of me, but if Sandra doesn't want to be involved with the co-op, she'll sell to whoever gives her the best offer."

Lucas shook his head. "There aren't many people who can afford a million-dollar property."

"Sandra is independently wealthy, Lucas. She paid cash

for the building and all of the renovation work."

He wished he'd known that before he'd spoken with the Realtor.

"I appreciate you wanting to look out for me but I don't need a man deciding how I should go about achieving my dream."

Shoot, he'd just been trying to help. He was a business-man and he solved problems for a living. She climbed out of the booth and he scrambled to his feet. "Let me walk you to your car."

"No, you stay here and say your goodbyes to Virginia and her husband."

"Are we still on for ice-skating tomorrow?"

She stopped, her hand on the door and for a second he was worried she intended to cancel on him.

"One o'clock." Then she was gone.

Lucas watched Ava walk down the block to her car. He'd touched a nerve when she'd found out he was trying to manipulate the situation with Stan Mueller so that Ava got the better end of the deal.

Go figure. Just when a guy thought he knew a woman, she proved that he hardy knew her at all.

"If this is your first time on the ice, you sure skate like a pro." Ava tightened her grip on Lucas's hand as they skirted the edge of Miracle Lake. Tilly and Sophie had retreated to the warming house fifteen minutes ago and Ava appreciated having a few minutes alone with him.

"I spent a lot of time at the Tanglefoot roller rink when I was a teenager," he said. "It's almost the same thing."

Ava slowed down so she could catch her breath. "I didn't skate until Sophie and I moved to Marietta. Tilly said I had to learn to enjoy winter otherwise I'd be stuck indoors for nine months out of the year."

Lucas tucked her against him when a group of teenagers raced by and bumped Ava. "Did it work?" he asked.

"Did what work?"

"Did you learn to love the bitter cold?"

"I don't think I'll ever be a huge fan of cold weather." She laughed. "But I've learned not to let winter weather keep me from having fun."

They'd been at the lake forty-five minutes and Ava still hadn't figured out how to explain her rudeness at the diner yesterday. "Lucas, I owe you an apology."

"For what?" He slowed down and moved to the outer edge of the ice where it was less crowded.

"I got defensive yesterday at the diner and I lashed out at you. I'm sorry."

"Are you talking about the part where you accused me of interfering with your dream?"

She sighed. "Yes."

"Why did I strike a nerve?"

"Drew was the kind of man who took charge. It was his way or the highway. He thought he knew what was best for me. I get that men feel protective but when I look back on my marriage his actions didn't feel protective; they felt controlling."

A group of noisy teens playing crack the whip in the center of the ice drew her attention. "Sophie's only four, but I worry she'll grow up and be reckless like her father."

He chuckled. "Sophie's just like you," he said. "Smart and adorable. She'll make good decisions."

Ava appreciated his vote of confidence. "I fought Drew tooth and nail about taking online classes to earn my degree. It wasn't a matter of money because I received tuition assistance through the military; it was that Drew wanted me to be dependent on him for everything and he thought if I earned a college degree I'd be able to take care of myself."

"You won the argument."

"I did. But it took a toll on our marriage. I've never talked about it with Tilly but before Drew died we were barely speaking to each other. We slept in the same bed but that was it. Most nights he grabbed dinner out and on weekends he hung around his buddies." She tugged his sleeve. "I'm sorry I was rude. But I need to handle this co-op on my own. If Sandra doesn't accept my proposal then the women and I will find a different location."

"You're opening my eyes to a few things I didn't realize about myself, Ava."

"What do you mean?"

"I loved my mother but the older I grew the more she needed my advice and help making decisions. After I graduated from college, there was a subtle shift in our relationship and my mom began delegating responsibilities to me like taking care of filing her taxes." He sent Ava a sad smile.

"Before she died I was doing everything for her." He slowed to a stop. "I offered to help you because I care about you, not because I don't believe you are capable of handling your own affairs."

Lucas's eyes were bluer than the sky and Ava felt herself falling. It would be so easy to let him have free rein with her heart but their lives were on parallel tracks heading in different directions.

"Can you skate backward?" he asked.

She skated ahead of him then turned and faced forward, swinging her hips side-to-side.

"Backward looks good on you." He grinned. "My turn." Lucas sped ahead of Ava then spun. He held out his hands and she grasped them.

"You're going a little fast," she said. "Be careful. You might trip."

"You'll save me."

His warm smile tugged at her heart. They'd known each other only six days—hardly enough time to fall in love. Even so he'd managed to carve out a tiny piece of her heart for himself. An image of him reading to Sophie flashed before her eyes, reminding Ava that her daughter's well-being came before hers. "When did you say you were heading back to California?"

He faced forward and fell in line with her. "That's the second time you've asked since we arrived at the lake." He smiled. "Are you in a hurry to get rid of me?"

"I'm sorry," she said. "I've got so much on my mind, I can't think straight." the *so much on her mind* was Lucas.

"I'm not sure." His heated gaze zeroed in on her mouth. "I could easily be persuaded to stay a while."

"Oh, really? How?"

He held up a finger. "One kiss." His gaze settled on her mouth and she thought he intended to kiss her in front of a hundred witnesses but the moment vanished when a shout from across the rink broke the spell they'd been under.

"Tilly wants to make supper for you before you leave town, so be sure to give me a heads-up when the time comes."

He tightened his grip on her hand. "I'm not criticizing Tilly or being judgmental," he said, "but I noticed that your mother-in-law—"

"Talks to herself."

He nodded. "I thought there was someone else in the living room with us."

"Drew said he couldn't remember a time when his mother hadn't carried on conversations with herself."

"What do you think of her habit?"

"I don't make a big deal about it, because I don't want Sophie judging her grandmother like others in this town do."

"People have been mean to Tilly?" he asked.

"Not mean, but they talk behind her back. They use words like unstable or ditzy. The kids call her silly Tilly."

"Then it's good that she has you and Sophie."

Ava smiled. "It's us three girls against the world." She inched closer to Lucas and he put his arm around her waist. "Speaking of gossip," she said, "my co-workers have been asking why you were seen getting out of Officer Bliven's patrol car in front of Tilly's house."

"Scott offered me a ride when he spotted me in the street." Lucas led them to the edge of the lake and they walked across the snow to a bench and sat. "Officer Henry Stubben was on my mother's list."

"The name doesn't sound familiar."

"He left Marietta years ago. Scott searched the 911 log books for 1987 and found a call that Henry responded to, which he thought might have involved my mother."

"What kind of call?"

"A report of a suspicious person squatting in the basement of the Graff. Scott said that the hotel had been boarded up and closed to the public back then."

"Do you think it was your mother?"

He shrugged. "I'll probably never learn the truth."

"And you said your mom didn't talk much about her two years in Marietta?"

"A few comments here or there but she never went into detail."

"I'm sure that was a scary time in her life." Ava tugged on his coat sleeve. "You know what I think, Lucas Kendrick?"

His blue-eyed gaze bore into hers. "What do you think, Ava Moore?"

"You're a really great guy."

His face drew closer and the moment his lips touched hers a gust of chilly air blew in her face and she sucked in a quick breath. Lucas took advantage of her open mouth, deepening the kiss, and Ava shivered but not from the cold.

He ended the kiss then tucked a strand of loose hair beneath her knitted cap. "Let's fetch Sophie from the warming house. I promised I'd show her my dancing moves."

Ava laughed. "This I have got to see."

Ten minutes later Ava and Tilly occupied the bench by the lake and watched Lucas and Sophie skate. The lessons Sophie had taken over the summer at the indoor rink in Livingston had paid off. The little princess could skate forward and backward without wobbling.

"Lucas is a nice man," Tilly said.

"He is."

"I approve of him."

Ava's head snapped sideways.

"Not that you're looking for or need my consent to become involved with a man."

"We're not involved."

"Maybe you haven't slept with him yet, but you're involved." Tilly's eyes twinkled. "Lucas made pancakes with Sophie."

"What are you getting at?"

"Drew was tough inside like his father. Men like that aren't easy to live with." She patted Ava's knee. "Drew's father called himself a man's man. I called him old-fashioned. He believed women should stay home, raise kids, cook and clean. He never helped around the house and he made all the decisions."

That had been Ava's marriage to Drew.

"I'm partly to blame for my son growing up believing that's the way relationships between men and women were meant to be. I should have stood up for myself, but I always took the path of least resistance." She pointed to Lucas who held Sophie on his hip and pretended they were dancing. "You would never guess that those two aren't father and daughter."

Ava wasn't surprised her mother-in-law was playing matchmaker. This past year Tilly dropped several hints that Ava should date.

"What do you and Sophie have planned for tomorrow while I'm working?" Ava asked.

"We're taking down the Christmas tree."

"I can help."

"I'll let you help put away the decorations in the yard this spring when the snow melts."

"That won't be until April."

Tilly smiled. "Do you ever wish you were back in Louisiana?"

"Not anymore." Ava wouldn't trade the cold and snow for warmer winters if it meant leaving Marietta. She enjoyed living in a small town where people looked out for each other. Besides, she couldn't ask Sophie's grandmother to sell her home and move to a city where she wouldn't be able to walk places to shop or eat. Lucas lifted Sophie above his head and twirled her. Her daughter's squeals echoed across the lake and Ava laughed.

How could the wrong man bring so much joy into her life and Sophie's?

Chapter Nine

LUCAS OPENED THE door of the Copper Mountain Chocolate shop and ushered the Moore ladies inside. A wave of sweet-smelling chocolate hit him in the face and he breathed in the rich aroma. Sophie walked up to the candy counter and pressed her nose against the glass case, and exclaimed over the bite-size chocolate Christmas trees with red candy bows and white sprinkles.

"Hello, Sophie." The woman behind the counter smiled at Lucas. "Whose your new friend?"

"He's Mr. Lucas." Sophie looked at him. "Can I have a Christmas tree?"

Ava joined them. "Hi, Rosie."

"You have noses like my name." Rosie laughed. "Have you been out skating or sledding?"

"Skating," Ava said.

"And Mr. Lucas danced with me like a princess."

Rosie's eyebrows arched, her gaze swinging between Lucas and Ava.

"This is Lucas Kendrick," Ava said. "He's staying at the Graff."

Rosie nodded. "The Lucas Kendrick who wandered away from the hotel Tuesday night during the snowstorm?"

"I was fine." Maybe he should borrow a megaphone and walk up and down Main Street reassuring the citizens that he was of sound mind and body.

"The hotel staff told Lucas he needs to try Sage's famous hot cocoa," Ava said, rescuing Lucas from an interrogation.

Rosie winked. "You can't leave town without drinking a Copper Mountain hot chocolate." She pointed to the end of the counter where Tilly perused the candy. "Four hot cocoas?"

Lucas nodded. "And a dozen Christmas tree chocolates." He took out his wallet.

When Rosie set the cocoas on the counter, Tilly looked at Lucas and asked, "Did you get a shot of caramel in yours?"

"We don't usually put caramel in the hot chocolate," Rosie said, "but I can add a dollop, if you'd like." She took one of the cups and disappeared into the kitchen.

"How did you know I'm a caramel fan?"

Tilly waved a hand in the air. "I think you mentioned something about caramel the other day at my house."

He did?

"C'mon, Sophie, we'll find a table." Tilly carried their cocoas and followed Sophie.

Ava reached inside her purse, but he shook his head. "This is my treat."

"Thank you, Lucas." She took her drink, leaving him alone at the counter.

Rosie returned with his cocoa and rang up the purchase. "Twenty-six sixty-three." When he handed over thirty dollars, she said, "I heard you're a Californian."

He nodded. "San Diego."

"Montana is a long way from the ocean."

"It is."

She doled out his change. "Are you and Ava…a couple?"

Lucas mulled over the word *couple* and liked the sound of it. "We're friends," he said. "Nice to meet you, Rosie." He grabbed his cocoa and the treats then joined the ladies at their table.

"Rosie's a talker," Ava said.

"Yes, she is." Lucas glanced around the shop. "The place is a lot bigger inside than I thought it would be."

"This past October the store closed for renovations," Ava said. "When it re-opened in November, Sage hired an apprentice chocolatier."

"I think his name is Avery," Tilly said. "He used to be a rodeo cowboy."

"Mommy, Mr. Lucas said I'm the first princess he ice-skated with."

"We don't have princesses in San Diego." Lucas held Ava's gaze, wondering if she felt things changing between them like he did. In his mind they'd shared a lot more than a few kisses since New Year's and he was having a heck of a time picturing himself driving away from this town and these ladies. He glanced at the chocolate treats. "Looks like the Christmas-tree candies were a hit."

"I saved you one, Mr. Lucas." Sophie offered him a chocolate-stained smile along with the treat.

"Thank you, princess." He popped the candy into his mouth. "Wow, this is pretty good."

"The red bows are mint-flavored," Ava said.

"This past June," Tilly explained, "the shop hosted a speed-dating event each Saturday and tested a new chocolate recipe with the daters." Tilly patted Ava's arm. "I couldn't persuade my daughter-in-law to sign up for the event."

Lucky for Lucas Ava hadn't attended the parties, otherwise she'd probably be with one of the bachelors right now.

Sophie talked about one of the little girls they'd met in the warming house and Lucas got a kick out of her animated facial expressions. As he listened with half an ear, he stole glances at Ava. A handful of days had passed since he'd first laid eyes on her in the hotel lobby after arriving in town and he'd spent most of his time since then thinking about her. Until now he hadn't gotten a clear picture of how he fit into Ava's life, but as he listened to the ladies chat he was certain anyone who saw them would believe they were a family.

"Mommy, can Mr. Lucas read me another bedtime story?"

Ava squirmed in her seat. "Honey, Mr. Lucas might have other plans tonight."

Might? It sounded as if Ava had left the door open to invite himself over. "My only plan is to return to my hotel room and check email." He winked at Sophie. "Reading the princess a story sounds like a lot more fun."

"Bedtime is early tonight, because I work tomorrow," Ava said.

"Do you work every Sunday?" he asked.

"One Sunday a month. It just so happened that New Year's fell on a Sunday this year and the housekeeping staff had to help with the fundraiser."

"What are your plans tomorrow, princess?" Lucas asked.

"I go to Nana's house." Sophie patted her grandmother's arm. "Nana, can Mr. Lucas come over and play?"

"We're taking down the Christmas tree," Tilly said. "Mr. Lucas can help us with the lights."

"I'd be happy to," he said.

Sophie chatted about her favorite ornaments on her grandmother's tree then Tilly mentioned that she had a light bulb in the hallway that had burned out and maybe Lucas could replace it for her. He suggested she make a to-do list for him to tackle while he was there.

Little by little Lucas was inserting himself into Ava's life. He knew it was risky. No one needed to hit him over the head with a brick to make him see that Sophie was growing attached to him, but he'd gotten caught up in feeling like part of their family. When he thought of saying goodbye to these ladies, he got a funny feeling in his chest—as if a vise was squeezing his heart.

Ask them to go back to San Diego with you.

He wished it were that simple. Ava had her co-op project—her dream. And her mother-in-law had a house in town. After admitting she'd adjusted to the cold weather, the California sunshine wouldn't be enough to entice Ava to move away.

You could move to Marietta.

He'd thought of that, but what kind of work could he find in the small town? After growing up without things and living on a shoestring budget he'd told himself he wouldn't settle for just scraping by. His position at Belfour Investments had come with a jump in pay. Besides if he gave up the job, he and his father would never move beyond being polite to each other.

"We better go." Ava stood. "Lucas, if you'd be kind enough to drop Tilly off at her house, Sophie and I will walk home."

"I'll drive you girls back to the apartment."

"We're just down the block." She smiled. "A bedtime story around seven-thirty would be perfect for Sophie."

"Sure." He gathered their trash and deposited the cups and candy wrappers in the garbage bin by the door. When they stepped outside Ava spoke first.

"Thank you for the hot chocolate and treats." She tapped her daughter's shoulder and Sophie chimed in with a thank you and so did Tilly.

"I'll see you tonight, princess." He turned to Tilly and said, "The pumpkin coach awaits, madam."

Sophie giggled.

Ava took Sophie's hand and as they walked off, Lucas heard the little girl ask, "Can you marry Mr. Lucas, Mommy?"

Ava kept walking, but Sophie looked over her shoulder and gave Lucas a little wave. The pip-squeak was tying his heartstrings into a giant knot. Now he understood why Sophie had interrogated him at the lake when they'd skated together. Did he like kids? Why didn't he have any kids? When was he going to have kids? Did he like girls better than boys? The princess had been interviewing him for a job—as her father.

Maybe some things didn't need to be contemplated, analyzed or evaluated. Maybe some things you just *knew*.

Like the fact that he was falling in love with Ava.

⇶⫷

"MR. LUCAS, LOOK." Sophie held up an ornament for his inspection.

"Is that Cinderella?" He stood on a stepladder in front of Tilly's Christmas tree early Sunday afternoon, attempting to untangle multiple strings of colored lights.

"Nana bought me Cinderella and the pumpkin coach." Sophie held up another ornament. "And this is Mr. Rat. He drives the pumpkin."

"Is there an evil stepmother?" he asked.

"There is." Tilly walked into the room. "But Ava wouldn't let me buy it because it wasn't Christmassy." She picked up a strand of lights Lucas had already untangled. "The tissue paper is on the dining-room table, Sophie. Make sure you wrap the ornaments before you put them into the bin."

Instead of doing as her grandmother had asked her to, Sophie played with the ornaments.

Lucas descended the stepladder and held out another strand of lights and Tilly secured the string with a plastic tie. "Thank you for helping me today, Lucas."

"My pleasure."

"The garland goes in this bin." She moved her knitting

bag to the couch and it toppled over, spilling balls of yarn and knitting needles onto the floor.

"I'll get them." He crouched down and collected the supplies, but stopped short of returning them to the bag when he saw the item Tilly was making.

"That's a cuddle cocoon," she said. "I knit them for the maternity ward at the hospital. Each newborn leaves in a blue or pink cocoon."

Lucas examined the pouch made out of blue yarn and swallowed hard. "I found one of these in my mother's things. It was light blue with tiny white turtles around the opening."

Tilly's eyes widened. "When were you born?"

"1987."

"I was knitting the cocoons then."

"My mom only kept a few of my baby mementos and the cocoon was one of them."

"I'm glad it meant so much to her." Tilly went over to the banister on the staircase and began removing the ornaments she'd hung on the garland. "You said you and your mother left Marietta to go back to San Diego. Didn't she contact your father at that time?"

He glanced at Sophie, making sure little ears weren't paying attention to the adult conversation. "My dad was married and had two sons when he got my mother pregnant with me."

Tilly glanced to her right and said, "That's terrible."

"She was nineteen at the time. My mom didn't talk about the past but she did say once that she was as much at fault as my father." He released the ties that secured the garland to the banister then fed Tilly a few feet at a time as she placed it into a plastic bin.

"Do you enjoy working for your father?"

Lucas mulled over the question for a few seconds then answered, "I do." Before meeting Roger, he'd been determined to keep his guard up, but then he'd looked into his father's eyes when they shook hands and the earnest sincerity in them had won Lucas over. But he doubted Roger had anticipated the blowback from his family.

Tilly pointed to the strand of lights strung over the doorway leading into the dining room and Lucas went to take them down.

"I wish my half brothers were more open to getting to know me."

"They appreciated the Padres tickets," Tilly said.

Lucas gaped at her. "How did you know I purchased baseball tickets for them?"

Her eyes widened and she turned away, fussing with the nativity display on the coffee table. "Isn't that what all men do when they want to keep the peace? Give away tickets to sporting events?"

It was odd that she knew the name of San Diego's professional baseball team. "Do you follow sports?"

"I watched a baseball game or two when my husband was alive."

"My brothers took the tickets but their attitude toward me didn't change."

Tilly swatted the air by her head and mumbled something unintelligible. The grandma was definitely eccentric, but her quirks made her sweet. Besides, he didn't care if she seemed distracted while they talked, because being around Tilly made him feel closer to his mother.

"You deserved a father growing up." She glanced over her shoulder at Sophie. "Every child needs two parents."

"Life doesn't always work out the way it should," he said. "I never learned how to throw a baseball, but I can make a mean meatloaf."

"There's nothing wrong with a man who knows his way around the kitchen."

⫸⫷

"AVA, I HAVE a favor to ask." Angelica stepped into the laundry room Sunday afternoon. "I know your shift just ended, but will you deliver this dry cleaning order to the guest's room before you leave? I forgot I have a meeting with David in five minutes."

"Sure," she said. "Can I get a favor in return?"

"What's that?"

"While you're talking with David, will you ask him if it's okay for me to give Lucas a tour of the hotel basement?"

"Why would you want to go down there?"

"Officer Bliven offered Lucas information that suggested his mother might have taken shelter in the basement back in the late eighties when she first arrived in town." Ava had felt so helpless when she'd watched Lucas's facial expressions as Virginia Pritchard told stories about his mother. She wanted to do something to help him and she thought if he saw the basement, he wouldn't have to imagine what it looked like when he thought of his mother.

"When did you want to take him down there?" Angelica asked.

"He's helping Tilly with her Christmas tree. I could call him after I deliver the laundry and see if he can get over here in a few minutes."

"Go ahead. I'll let David know but I'm sure he'll be fine with it." Angelica winked. "Be careful."

"Why do you say that?"

"The ghost questers from the show *Ghost Quest* didn't find anything conclusive back in October when they explored the hotel, but that doesn't mean there aren't lost souls wandering around this building."

"You don't believe in ghosts, do you?"

Angelica lowered her voice. "When I first began working here, I went into the attic several times searching for one thing or another and it always smelled as if someone had just smoked a cigar up there."

The comment reminded Ava of the morning she'd waited for Sandra to arrive in her dress shop and she'd caught a whiff of tobacco when she'd inspected the chair in the display window.

"Now that I think about it," Angelica said, "I went into the attic several times searching for decorations for New Year's Eve and there was no cigar odor." She shrugged. "Maybe the ghost hunters chased the spirit out of the hotel."

Or maybe the tobacco ghost had gone along for the ride when the old hotel chair had been delivered to Sandra's store.

"Thanks for taking care of the dry cleaning." Angelica waved and disappeared down the hallway.

Ava checked the tag on the laundry—311. Lucas's room. Had this been a coincidence or was Angelica playing matchmaker again? Ava rode the elevator to the third floor. She followed protocol and knocked on Lucas's door. "Housekeeping."

She waited a few seconds and knocked a second time—just in case one of the guests was spying on her through their peephole. "Housekeeping, Mr. Lucas—I mean, Mr. Kendrick." She keyed into the room and flipped on the light. The staff had been by earlier in the day and had made up his bed. The curtains had been opened and his trash emptied. She walked over to the mirrored closet door to hang up his laundry and froze when she saw the picture taped to the door.

Lucas had taped up the picture Sophie had made for him when he'd spent the night at their apartment. She studied the drawing, smiling at the crowns on top of their heads. When she noticed that the stick figures held hands her eyes burned. She hung the laundry in the closet and slid the door closed. All along she'd second-guessed herself and worried that she was falling too hard and too fast for Lucas. It was one thing for Ava to get her heart broken but she had to protect her daughter's heart, too.

After she showed Lucas the basement it was time to take a step back. She'd gotten caught up in the whirlwind of her attraction to him and the magic of their New Year's kiss but real life wasn't a fairy tale and it was time Ava began thinking with her head and not her heart.

She returned to the employee break room and texted Lucas to meet her at the hotel then went into the lobby to wait for him.

Ava spotted the rental car when it pulled into the parking lot. Before Lucas reached the lobby door, a beautiful woman cut him off. They stood outside and chatted for a minute then Lucas held the door open for her. A sliver of jealousy pricked Ava when the lady touched his arm before walking into the bar. Lucas was a great catch—a good-looking, confident, successful businessman. And what Ava knew, which the other woman did not, was that Lucas was also generous, patient, and caring, which made it all the more difficult to keep her defenses up around him.

When he noticed her across the room, he smiled and her insides melted like a stick of butter in a microwave. He walked over and gave her a hug. "Thank you, Ava. This means so much to me." He took off his coat.

"We may not find any proof that your mother—"

"I know," he said, still smiling. "Lead the way."

They took the service elevator and as soon as they stepped inside, Lucas made a move to kiss her. The image of Sophie's drawing popped into Ava's head and she shifted away from him, wincing at the surprised look in his eyes. A moment later the elevator stopped and the doors opened.

She flipped the switch on the wall. "The lighting isn't great down here but at least we won't walk into walls."

"This place is creepy," he said. "The hotel's been renovated but it looks like they kept a few of the limestone walls."

"They moved the laundry facilities to the first floor, but left the hotel's original wine cellar down here." She pointed to their right where a pair of massive double doors waited at the end of the hallway. "That's off-limits."

"I'd like to figure out which room had the window Officer Stubben reported seeing lit up that night."

They entered the room across from the elevator first. Ava pointed above their heads where hooks had been screwed into the wooden beams crisscrossing the ceiling. "I bet they stored dried meats and vegetables in here when the hotel first opened."

"There's no window." Lucas took her hand and she let him. "The report mentioned a window on the north side of the hotel." He walked around the elevator to the other side of the basement and they entered a room where sunlight streamed through a window along the top of one wall. A cold breeze ushered them farther into the room. "My mother was a petite woman. She could have fit through that window."

"How would she have climbed back out?" Ava asked.

"Maybe there was a a table or chair in the room basement that she stood on to reach the window."

Ava ran her fingers over the smooth limestone walls. Masonries had spent endless hours fitting rocks together before setting them in place with mortar. Her fingers skimmed across deep gouges in the stone. "Do you have your cell phone on you?"

"Yeah. Why?"

"If you have a flashlight app on the phone, shine the

light over here."

Lucas pointed the light at the wall. "Those look like letters scratched into the surface of the stone."

"The wall was probably damaged during the renovation work."

"I'll be back." Ava rode the elevator to the lobby and stopped at the front desk. "Bob, will you please hand me a sheet of computer paper and a pencil?"

"Sure. What's going on?"

"Nothing." Ava smiled. "Just making a to-do list." She dashed back to the elevator. When she joined Lucas in the basement again, she said, "Hold the light steady." She placed the sheet of paper over the abrasions and lightly ran the pencil lead across the surface.

Lucas sucked in a loud breath when the letter C appeared on the paper. Then A R O L. "My mother's name."

"There's more." Ava moved the paper to the right and repeated the process. When she finished, she read the message out loud. "Carol K 1987."

Lucas's gaze flicked between the wall and the paper.

Thinking he might like some privacy, Ava said, "I'll wait for you by the elevator."

"Stay." There was such sadness in his eyes that her heart broke for him. He sank to the floor against the wall and she joined him.

"I can't believe my mother sought shelter in an abandoned hotel."

He wrapped his arms around his bent knees. "It's difficult to believe the man who rejected me and my mom is the same man I'm now working for."

Ava wished she could do more than offer quiet support.

He shook his head. "Why would my mom want me to have a relationship with a man who was living a good life while she'd been forced to hide out in an abandoned building? It doesn't make sense."

"Maybe there's something she couldn't or wouldn't tell you."

"That doesn't excuse my father for not taking responsibility for his actions. My mother's life was hard, Ava. There weren't any vacations. She never owned her own home. She drove used cars."

Ava squeezed his fingers. "Maybe so, Lucas, but you made up for any hardship she went through. You were her biggest blessing in life."

"I was a huge responsibility."

Ava shook her head. "I'm speaking from experience when I say the bond between a mother and her child is stronger than anything else in the world. You were all that mattered to your mom. As long as she had you…she had everything."

"She told me that she'd intended to give me up for adoption after I was born, but she said she changed her mind when the people in town reached out to help her." He leaned his head against the wall and closed his eyes. "If her bus money hadn't run out in Marietta, I might not be here." He looked at Ava. "I feel like Marietta was my mother's home and San Diego was just a place we lived." He leaned his head against the wall and closed his eyes. "I know one thing for sure."

"What's that?"

"I came here for answers and all I've ended up with are more questions." He looked at Ava. "Nothing makes sense. Except you."

She wondered how many times a person's heart could melt before it became useless. After meeting Lucas only seven days ago Ava knew more about him than she had about Drew after two years of marriage to him.

Perhaps time was meaningless and the heart just knew when *the one* came along?

Chapter Ten

"THANKS AGAIN, TOD," Lucas said, unbuckling his seat belt after the Realtor parked in front of the Graff Hotel. They'd spent most of Monday afternoon checking out a 1920s' Methodist church building that was for sale on the outskirts of Bozeman.

"I'll keep looking for properties," Tod said. "Let me know when you hear back from your client whether we're keeping this on the list or not."

"Will do." Lucas had emailed photos and a brief description of the building to Stan Mueller while they'd toured the property and Lucas had yet to hear back from the man.

"Good afternoon, sir." Ron held open the lobby door.

Lucas pulled off his gloves and unzipped his coat. "How's your day going?"

"Fine, sir." The bellman's eyes darted toward the check-in desk. He lowered his voice. "That gentlemen asked if I knew your whereabouts, sir."

A man Lucas's height with short gray hair stood chatting with Bob. *No way.* He walked over to the desk. "Roger?" He didn't know what shocked him more—that his father had traveled to a state like Montana or that the man was grinning. "What are you doing here?"

Roger's smile slipped. "I decided I needed a break from the family, too."

What was going on? Roger lived and breathed Belfour Investments. He wouldn't have left the office unless he was traveling on business.

"Mr. Belfour," Bob said. "You'll be in room 309." The desk clerk nodded to Lucas as if he'd done him a favor by assigning Roger to the room next to his. "Sir, would you like Ron to take your luggage to the room?"

"I would, thank you." Roger dropped a ten-dollar bill on the counter. "For the bellman." He looked at Lucas. "Join me for a drink?"

Eager to find out the purpose of Roger's visit, Lucas said, "This way." They entered the turn-of-the-century bar with its elegant wood paneling and hammered copper ceiling. Lucas had visited the pub twice since he'd checked in to the hotel and knew the female bartender by her first name. At this hour the place was deserted.

"Good afternoon, gentlemen."

"How are you, Shane?"

"Fine, Mr. Kendrick. Your usual?" She placed drink napkins on the bar.

Shane was a confident, no-nonsense woman who wasn't afraid to look a person in the eye. He could easily imagine her as a corporate executive and didn't understand why she tended bar in a rural town.

"I'm in the mood for a working man's beer." He ignored his father's surprised glance. Lucas hadn't been a beer-drinker since college, but he felt compelled to remind Roger that although he was his son, they came from vastly different worlds.

"And for you, sir?" She looked at Roger.

"Scotch on the rocks."

Shane delivered their drink orders and then placed a bowl of shelled peanuts on the bar. "Would you care for menus?"

"No, thank you," Lucas said.

"Not yet," Roger added.

Shane must have sensed the tension between Lucas and Roger because she retreated to the far end of the bar and kept herself busy.

Lucas tossed a few nuts into his mouth then took a swig of beer and grimaced. He'd forgotten he'd drunk the fizzy brew in college because it had been cheap, not because he'd liked the taste.

Lucas decided he'd break the ice. "What's going on with your family that you felt the need to get away?"

"I don't know why I said that." Roger sipped his scotch. "Or maybe I do."

Lucas studied his father's hunched shoulders— uncharacteristic of the confident, commanding businessman he worked for. Roger downed the rest of his scotch then pushed the glass away and spun his stool so he faced Lucas. "I came to apologize."

Before the words had a chance to sink in Shane walked over. "Would you like another, sir?"

Roger nodded at Lucas. "Bring him a scotch, too." He sent Lucas a wry smile. "You look like you could use something stronger."

When Lucas discovered he and his father preferred scotch, he'd been surprised, especially after his half brothers said they preferred martinis—another reason for Brady and Seth to resent Lucas.

Shane returned with their drinks and removed the half-empty beer bottle in front of Lucas before leaving them to their conversation.

The word *apologize* was still ricocheting inside Lucas's head when his father continued speaking.

"I'm ashamed to admit I haven't handled things well since you've joined the company." He shook his head. "No, that's not it. I came to say that I'm sorry I didn't stand up to Claire and tell her to go jump off the Santa Monica Pier when she railed against you after the Christmas party."

"I shouldn't have drunk so much."

Roger's mouth curved into a wry smile. "If not for alcohol I'd have been divorced years ago."

Lucas chuckled.

"I haven't handled things well since you came to work for me. I want you to know that I'm going to try harder."

"I never intended to make your family life more difficult."

"This is my doing, not yours. And you shouldn't be treated as if you were the one who did something wrong." Roger held up his hand. "Don't think I haven't noticed the effort you're making to prove yourself. You're a brilliant young man and a hard worker." He shook his head. "You outperform Seth and Brady in every category and I'm not talking about your business experience and work ethic." He nodded. "I mean your character."

Lucas stared into his drink glass, wondering if he needed to have his hearing tested.

"Since you left town, I've been doing some serious soul searching and I'm embarrassed to admit that I've held back defending you to my family, because it's been difficult for me to accept the truth."

"What truth?"

"That I can't claim credit for the fine young man you've become."

Lucas drained his scotch, blaming the burning sensation in his eyes on the alcohol stinging his throat. "I don't know what I'm supposed to say."

"You don't have to say anything. I'll do all the talking." Roger took a sip of his scotch. "I know why you chose to visit Montana."

Lucas's eyes narrowed.

"What do you say we move to one of those booths and order something to eat? I suspect we'll have had a few too many drinks by the time we're finished with this conversation."

Now that the moment had finally arrived and Roger appeared ready to answer the questions that had nagged Lucas for years, he wasn't sure he was prepared to hear the truth. He loved his mother. Loved her for the sacrifices she'd made for him and he worried that what Roger had to say would change his memories of her.

I want you to contact your father.

His mother wouldn't have asked that of him, if she didn't want him to know the truth. Lucas waved at Shane. "We'll order food."

They sat in a booth and Shane dropped off the menus and two glasses of water. "If you like seafood, I recommend the house fish sandwich. Deep-fried, beer-batter cod served on a ciabatta roll, with slaw and fries."

"I'll have that," Roger said.

"Same here."

"It'll be ready in a jiffy." Shane turned away but Roger's voice stopped her. "Miss," he said. "Keep the scotch coming."

"I'll do better than that." She walked behind the bar and retrieved a bottle of Lagavulin then set it on their table before walking off to give the cook their orders.

"What do you know about Marietta?" Lucas asked.

"I know it's the town you and your mother lived in for two years after she gave birth to you."

"Why—"

Roger held up his hand cutting Lucas off. "Before I go any further, did your mother explain how we knew each other?"

"No."

"She was our babysitter. Claire and I moved into a starter home down the block from your grandparents' house. Claire asked if she babysat and Carol began watching the boys."

Lucas was stunned. "You slept with your babysitter?"

Roger's face turned red. "She was eighteen—not that I'm excusing my behavior." He released a deep sigh. "Your mother's parents were hard people, Lucas. Your grandmother barely spoke to the neighbors and hid in the house all the time. Your grandfather was a cold man who had nothing nice to say about anyone. I felt bad for Carol and your grandmother. I believe your grandfather verbally abused them." Roger stared at his scotch and Lucas waited for him to continue.

"Claire and I came home from a dinner party one Saturday night. She drove because I'd had too much to drink. When your mother babysat for us I'd always walk her back to her house if it was dark outside. That night your grandparents were out of town for a funeral."

Roger's shoulders sunk lower. "I'm not making excuses," he said. "I'm just telling you how I justified my actions back then." He looked at Lucas. "Like I said I'd had too much to drink and Claire and I argued on the way home from the party. We did a lot of bickering early on in our marriage. Your mother must have sensed I wasn't eager to get back to Claire because she invited me inside."

Lucas was glad his father was having a difficult time talking about the past. Lucas would have found it more troubling if he hadn't.

"We talked for a while. I asked her how school was going. Then out of the blue Carol leaned over and kissed me." Roger shook his head. "I should have left right then but I didn't. When I snuck home an hour later, Claire was waiting for me in the kitchen."

"She knew."

Roger nodded. "I expected her to ask for a divorce."

Obviously Claire hadn't because they were still married.

"I'd just started my company and a divorce would have bankrupted my business."

"What did she say?"

His father sat up straight and stuck his chest out. "'Roger, I want the house on Fifth Avenue,' then she went up to bed."

"A house?"

"Claire had fallen in love with a home in an upscale neighborhood where one of her friends lived. Status was more important to her than my fidelity."

"You bought her the house."

Roger finished his scotch then poured a refill and topped off Lucas's glass. "I was only thinking of myself. I didn't want one mistake to ruin my business. I bought the house and Claire and I never spoke of that night again."

"Until my mother told you she was pregnant."

"Not even then. Claire didn't know I'd gotten Carol pregnant until you showed up at my office."

At least now Lucas better understood why Claire was less than welcoming when they'd met. She'd believed her husband's mistake was behind them only to be faced with it again decades later.

"I came clean after the Christmas party and told Claire that I'd given your mother money to leave town after I found out she was pregnant." Roger stared into space. "At the time I'd convinced myself that I was doing Carol a favor by offering her the means to get away from your grandfather."

"And Claire still hasn't asked for a divorce?"

"She'll never walk away from me. She likes our lifestyle too much. Seth and Brady took Claire's side and they should. I'm the one who did their mother wrong."

"Here you go, gentlemen." Shane arrived with their food. "Ketchup, mustard, relish and hot sauce are on the table." She pointed to the bottles. "Anything else I can get for you?"

Roger shook his head and Lucas, said, "We're fine, thanks, Shane."

Conversation stopped for a few minutes while they sampled their fish sandwiches and Lucas mulled over what he'd learned about his parents' relationship. Now he understood why his mother had said she was as much at fault as Roger for her getting pregnant.

"Even though my mom made the first move," Lucas said, "you were ten years older. Inebriated or not, you should have known better."

"You're right and I regretted sending Carol away. That's why I hired a private eye to track her down."

"You knew she ended up in Marietta."

Roger nodded. "By the time the man had located Carol you were six months old. She was working at the diner in town and you two lived in the Sunset Apartments on First Avenue." Roger set his sandwich on the plate and wiped his mouth with a napkin. "Claire never knew that I kept track of you all these years."

"What do you mean all these years?"

"Your mother was a strong woman, a hard worker and proud."

"How do you know?"

"I sent her a check every month but she never cashed them."

Stunned Lucas stared unseeing into space remembering all the years his mother had struggled to make ends meet. Was her pride more important than providing for her child? Even though they had a roof over their heads and food on the table, they could have enjoyed life more if she'd cashed Roger's checks. She could have bought herself a new car or she could have paid for the science camp he'd wanted to go to in the sixth grade. Instead he'd sat home that week by himself while all of his friends were off having fun.

"I decided if I was going to help you and your mother she couldn't know about it."

"What did you do?"

"The manager of the bank where your mother worked was a friend of mine. He hired Carol as a favor to me."

No wonder his mother had been the only teller without a college degree. "What else did you do?"

Roger shifted his gaze to the wall of liquor bottles behind the bar. "Whatever I did it wasn't enough."

"I'd like to know."

"Your scholarship at ASU was paid for by Belfour Investments."

Lucas had thought he'd received the tuition assistance because of his mother's income and having grown up in a single-parent household.

"My money was better spent on you than Brady and Seth. You've done well for yourself, Lucas. You quickly moved up the ladder at G&H Grocery after you began working there. I can't tell you how many times I'd walk into Seth or Brady's office and wish you were sitting in their chairs." He offered a rueful smile. "Some days I think they wish that, too."

"What do you mean?"

"They take after Claire more than me. They've lived a pampered life and don't know the meaning of hard work. They partied in college, earned liberal arts degrees, which are useless in the business world, and then they couldn't find jobs after they graduated so I hired them."

"What would Seth and Brady rather be doing?"

"Seth wanted to be an artist."

Lucas had no idea. "What kind of art?"

"Painting. Claire's grandfather was a portrait artist and Seth inherited his artistic genes. And Brady would be happy working on an assembly line if he could find a manufacturing job. He's not a problem solver."

All this time Lucas believed his half brothers were acting territorial because they didn't like their father's attention on Lucas when maybe they were just jealous that Lucas was doing what he loved and they weren't.

"Why don't you let Brady and Seth chase their dreams and hire someone to replace them?"

"I've thought about it, but I'm trying to grow the company and…"

"And what?"

Roger stared Lucas in the eye. "I don't know if you'll stick around." He rushed on. "Belfour Investments is a small company and it won't be long before larger, more successful firms come knocking at your door."

Lucas soaked in the praise. He'd always yearned to have a father's respect and now that he did, he admitted it felt pretty darn good.

"Carol never married," Roger said. "Was she happy being single?"

"There were times in her life when she was lonely," Lucas said. "But we were close." He nodded. "How did you end up with Claire?"

"We met in college. Claire was attracted to me because her parents didn't approve of my middle-class background and I'd never dated a girl who came from money." Roger smiled. "Neither of our families was happy about our marriage."

"Did Claire's parents ever find out that you'd cheated on her with my mother?"

Roger shook his head. "A year before things happened with Carol, Claire had convinced her father to bankroll my company and that's how I was able to get it off the ground. She stayed with me because she didn't want to have to listen to her father's I-told-you-so if we divorced."

Lucas liked knowing that his father came from a middle-class family—it made him seem more human and maybe a little easier to forgive.

Forgive. Is that what he was doing?

"I've done a lot of things I'm not proud of in my life, Lucas. How I handled the situation with your mother is one of my biggest regrets."

Roger looked Lucas in the eye. "My apology probably

doesn't mean much to you, but I'm offering it nonetheless."

Unable to speak because of the knot in his throat, Lucas sipped from his water glass. When he'd regained his composure, he asked, "How long are you staying?"

"A couple of days if you don't object. I'd like to learn more about the town that took Carol in when I left her out in the cold."

"I'd be happy to give you a tour of Marietta." Lucas looked forward to showing Roger around.

They finished eating then his father paid for their meals and the bottle of scotch before announcing that he was turning in early.

It would be a while before Lucas made sense of everything he'd learned. But tonight Roger had given him hope that the father-son relationship he'd yearned for all his life was within reach.

Lucas was too wired to sleep and as soon as he returned to his room he pulled out his phone to call Ava. His finger froze above her number on the screen. He sat on the end of the bed and stared at the drawing Sophie had made for him. The first person he'd thought of sharing this incredible feeling with had been Ava. He was taken aback by how important she'd become to him. It was close to Sophie's bedtime but maybe Ava would be up for a quick visit. He texted her a message, volunteering to read the little princess a bedtime story then went into the bathroom and brushed his teeth. Ava returned his text a few minutes later.

Princess Sophie says she'll be waiting for you in the castle courtyard.

Lucas shrugged into his coat, grabbed the rental keys from his briefcase then took the stairs to the lobby. Ron wasn't stationed at the door, so he escaped the hotel without having to say where he was going.

When he pulled up behind Ava's apartment, he was surprised to find several cars parked in the lot along with her Toyota. Maybe Sandra was meeting with her employees in the dress shop. He got out of the car and pressed the door lock.

"Mr. Lucas!"

He glanced up and spotted Sophie standing on the landing dressed in her pink footie pajamas, winter boots, coat, hat, scarf and mittens. Grinning, he climbed the stairs. "What are you doing out here in the cold?"

She spread her arms wide. "Waiting for you."

His heart smiled.

"It's gonna be noisy."

"Why's that?" he asked.

"Mommy's ladies are here."

Ladies? He opened the door and ushered Sophie inside where a group of women were gathered around the kitchen island. As soon as they noticed him, they stopped talking.

"Ladies, this is Lucas Kendrick," Ava said.

"He's a prince," Sophie announced. "And he's gonna read me a bedtime story."

The women glanced between Lucas and Ava, obviously wondering about their relationship.

"I didn't mean to interrupt," he said.

"We're meeting about the co-op." Ava walked over and

offered to take his coat. He was disappointed that she wasn't alone but smiled and said, "I'll make it quick."

"No need to rush," Ava said. "We're wrapping things up." She helped Sophie get out of her winter gear then the pip-squeak ran off to her room.

Lucas skirted the edge of the group. "I'll let you ladies get back to work." He disappeared into Sophie's bedroom, closing the door partway.

"Are you ready, Mr. Lucas?"

"I'm ready, Princess Sophie. What are we reading to-night?"

She held up the book. *"Can't You Sleep Little Bear?"*

A cold blast of air swept over Lucas and he glanced at the window, but it was closed tight. He sat on Sophie's bed and opened the book. "My mom used to read me this story when I was a little boy."

"She did?"

The moment Lucas had arrived in Marietta he'd felt there was something different…almost magical about the town. As if Marietta was more than just the place he'd been born in. He breathed deeply through his nose and exhaled slowly through his mouth, loosening the knot in his chest. "Okay, I'm ready. Are you?"

She snuggled under his covers, holding her teddy bear close. "Now I'm ready."

Lucas took his time reading the story and when he said "The End" and closed the book, Sophie was sound asleep. Gently he removed her glasses and set them on the nightstand then turned off the light. He sat for a while longer on the bed, staring at her cute little face, imagining her growing older, becoming a teenager, and then a young lady heading off to college to find her place in the world. Every little girl needed a daddy to protect her. Before his imagination got the best of him, he brushed Sophie's bangs out of her eyes and placed a kiss on the top of her head then quietly left the little princess to her dreams.

When he stepped out of Sophie's bedroom the apartment was empty. A few seconds later the door opened and Ava entered and hung her coat up on the hook by the door.

"They didn't leave because of me, did they?"

"No." She waved off his concern then began collecting the papers that were strewn all over the island.

"How did your meeting go?" he asked.

"We were discussing a promotion campaign."

"Did Sandra get back to you about your proposal?" He sat down at the counter.

"I'm stopping by her house tomorrow before I go into work." Ava frowned. "Has she spoken to you about the store?"

He shook his head. "I'd planned to contact her, but I'll hold off until after you two."

Ava set the papers aside, and studied him. "How are you doing after our trip to the basement?"

The past two days had been emotional for Lucas and he appreciated Ava's concern. "I texted you tonight because I needed to talk to you."

She smiled. "You could have called."

"I wanted to tell you in person."

Her smile faded. "What happened?"

"My father's in town."

Her eyes widened. "Were you expecting him?"

"He surprised me."

"Did he say why he's here?"

Lucas nodded. "He came because he felt bad that he let his wife exile me."

"He apologized."

"Ava."

"What?"

"He wants to make up for the past."

"How do you feel about that?"

He smiled. "I think I'm ready."

Ava nibbled her lip, and he asked, "What's wrong?"

"Nothing. I'd just hate to see you get hurt."

"We had a long talk after he got here. There's a lot to forgive but if I don't give him a chance, I'll never know what could have been."

"You have to do what you believe is best."

"I'd like you to meet him."

She shook her head. "I don't think—"

"It would mean a lot to me if you and Sophie would have dinner with us at the hotel tomorrow night." He valued Ava's instincts and knew she'd tell him if she believed his father was pulling the wool over his eyes.

"What time?" she asked.

"Six."

"We'll be there."

Lucas felt all the tension leave his body and it didn't escape him that Ava was the reason for his contentedness. When he was with her, he didn't feel adrift—she was his anchor.

Chapter Eleven

TUESDAY MORNING AFTER dropping Sophie off at preschool, Ava parked her car on the street in front of Sandra and the judge's home on Bramble Lane. She hoped her landlord had good news for her.

Ava hadn't gotten a wink of sleep last night after Lucas had left the apartment. He'd been excited to share the news that his father had flown in to Montana for a surprise visit, but she worried that Roger had an ulterior motive and tonight at dinner she'd learn what kind of man he was.

She grabbed the co-op file off the passenger seat and stepped from the car. Although it was bitterly cold, the winds from yesterday had died down and the air sparkled from the sun's rays reflecting off the snow—hopefully a good omen.

Ava climbed the porch steps and banged the iron knocker. The door opened a moment later. "Good morning." Sandra waved her into the foyer then took Ava's jacket and hung it on an ornate coat hook mounted to the wall.

"I haven't been in the house since you replaced all the drapes with plantation shutters."

"Updating this old home has been a challenge, but Elena and I are making progress." Sandra smiled. "Alistair lets his great-granddaughter talk him into anything so I tell Elena what I want and she convinces Alistair it's her idea and he caves in."

Ava laughed. "Sounds like a great system."

"It's worked on every room so far except his office."

"Speaking of the judge," Ava said, "I didn't see Cat hanging around the porch."

Sandra pointed at the staircase behind her. The scraggly, yellow-eyed tom with half of one ear missing sat on the bottom step.

"I thought the stray refused to come in the house?" According to Sandra the cat lived beneath the front porch all year.

"Alistair keeps a basement window open during the winter so Cat can crawl inside if he gets too cold. Unbeknownst to me, the grumpy feline has been joining Alistair for breakfast before I come downstairs in the morning."

"How long has this been going on?"

"A while. I might never have known if Alistair hadn't accidentally closed the basement door, trapping the little monster inside the house with me this morning." The women stared at the animal, his tail swishing back and forth as if he knew they were discussing him.

"He won't go back outside?"

"I opened the basement door for him but he hasn't budged from that step."

"He's probably waiting for his master to return."

"We'll chat in Alistair's office since he's at the courthouse this morning."

Ava followed Sandra down the hallway, feeling the snaggle-toothed little monster yellow glare burning the back of her head. When she entered the judge's office, she stepped back in time to the late sixties. The pea-green walls and mustard-colored drapes clashed with the burnt orange rug covering the wood floor. Several landscape paintings hung in the room and behind the judge's massive mahogany desk rows of bookshelves took up an entire wall. She bet the judge had read every one of the books.

Sandra crossed the room to a drink cart in front of the window. "I made a pot of coffee. Would you like a cup?"

"I'd love one, thanks."

"Sugar or cream?"

"Black is fine." Ava sat in one of the leather chairs facing the desk. "Thank you," she said when Sandra set the cup on the table beside Ava.

Sandra returned to the cart and poured herself a cup. "Good grief."

"What's the matter?"

"I just saw Gladys peeking through her blinds at me."

Sandra sat at the judge's desk. "Alistair warned me about that woman after we married. Apparently she's been the neighborhood watchdog for years. She and Alistair's wife were best friends." Sandra sipped her coffee. "In the summer the ladies would gossip over the hedge while they hung their husbands' tighty-whities on the clothesline to dry."

Ava laughed then stopped abruptly when Lucas popped into her mind. What kind of underwear did he prefer—briefs or boxers?

"Well," Sandra said. "Let's talk business."

"I'm assuming you've heard back from your lawyer."

"I did." Sandra frowned and Ava's stomach dropped to her toes. "He advised against a partnership with the co-op."

"Did he give a reason why?"

"Many. However, I've decided not to take his advice."

"You have? Why?"

"Donald is conservative and he never takes risks, which was fine when I was younger. But I'm not a spring chicken and it's time I took a few chances." She smiled. "I'm going to accept your proposal."

Ava let out a little scream of excitement in her head then she thought of Lucas and her joy fizzled. She wished there didn't have to be a loser in this deal. "All of us women in the co-op are hard workers, Sandra. You won't regret this." Ava leaned forward in the chair. "What swayed you?"

"Alistair." Sandra's gaze flicked to the doorway. "Please don't mention this to anyone, but he fell yesterday."

Ava gasped. "Is he okay?"

"He's fine. Thank goodness. He claims he was just clumsy but I've noticed the past few months that he doesn't pick his feet up when he walks. He shuffles and I think his shoe caught the edge of the carpet and he lost his balance." She sighed. "When I look at Alistair, I don't see how old he is. In my mind and heart he's a much younger man. But now I understand why he's been badgering me to cut back on my hours at the store. He's trying to tell me what I've refused to acknowledge—that he's slowing down."

"I'm glad he wasn't hurt, Sandra."

"Me, too. Anyway, I'll instruct my lawyer to draw up the necessary legal documents and find out if I need any special permits to house the co-op in my building."

"And the judge will be okay with your decision? I know he was pushing you to sell."

"As long as this partnership goes smoothly and I'm not drawn into the day-to-day problems at the dress shop, he'll be fine."

"What do you mean by day-to-day problems?"

"If we're going to do this, Ava, then I need someone reliable to manage the shop. I know you suggested that I train the women in the co-op to work in the store when I'm on vacation but after the scare I had with Alistair, I plan to spend all of my time with him. I don't want to deal with inventory, sales, or keeping the books."

"Did you have anyone in mind to take over?" Ava squirmed when Sandra's gaze pinned her. "Me?"

"Why not?"

"I don't know anything about ladies' fashion."

"You have a business degree."

"But no experience."

"Then you'll get experience when you run the dress shop." Sandra smiled. "I see a little bit of me in you. You're a go-getter, Ava. I can't picture you working at the Graff forever."

Ava couldn't, either. The housekeeping job had paid the bills while Ava earned her degree. It wasn't what she wanted to do forever.

"When and if the time comes..." Sandra blinked hard

then straightened her shoulders "…that I need to keep myself busy again, I'll help out with the dress shop."

"I don't know what to say." Ava nibbled her lip.

"You seem hesitant, dear."

"It's a great opportunity, Sandra, but managing both the co-op and the store is a lot of responsibility."

"I'll help you make the transition and I'm always available if you have questions."

Nothing ventured, nothing gained. And she couldn't disappoint the women in the co-op. "I'm in."

"Good. Alistair will be thrilled when I tell him at dinner tonight."

Ava stood. "Did you want me to break the news to Lucas?"

"I'll do that, dear. I'm sure he'll have questions." Sandra led the way to the front door. "I'll call him tomorrow morning."

Ava put on her coat then hugged Sandra. "Thank you."

"Make me proud, dear."

"I will."

As soon as the door closed behind her, Ava hurried down the porch steps and out to the car. She was at once terrified and excited. The ladies in the co-op would be thrilled when they heard the news. Lucas would not be thrilled.

What if he asked about her meeting with Sandra tonight? She'd cross that bridge when she came to it.

"WHAT'S ON TAP for today?" Roger asked.

Lucas and his father had just finished brunch in the hotel dining room and were lingering over coffee. "I have an errand to run at the library, would you like to come along?"

Roger quirked an eyebrow but before Lucas had a chance to explain, his phone rang. "Hello." It was Stan Mueller. He didn't want his father overhearing their conversation. "I need to take this call." He left the table and went to the lobby.

"How are you, Stan?" After they exchanged pleasantries, Stan said he appreciated Lucas searching for other properties but if the building in Marietta fell through he was moving on—no hard feelings. Either way he wanted an answer by the end of the week and Lucas assured him he'd have one.

"I thought you were on vacation?" Roger said when Lucas returned to the table. The waiter appeared and topped off their coffee cups.

"I'm mixing pleasure and business."

Roger traced his finger over the design in the tablecloth. "I was a go-getter at your age, too. Worked twelve-hour days, weekends, holidays."

One of the things Lucas had noticed when he'd first begun working at Belfour Investments was that his half brothers made a mad dash to the door at five o'clock, but Roger stayed until seven. "You work just as late as I do at the office."

"We don't have any privacy during the day and I thought if you ever had any questions about me or your mother we'd talk after everyone left."

THIRTY YEARS LATER his father had wanted to be there for him and Lucas wanted it, too, but trust didn't happen overnight.

What about Ava? Lucas hadn't known her long but he trusted her. "Roger, why are you really here?"

"I told you. I felt bad that I didn't stand up to Claire when she had a meltdown." His attention shifted to the window overlooking the parking lot. "I've always wanted to see the place that took you and Carol in, but I was too chicken to come by myself."

"Why?"

"I'm ashamed at how I treated your mother. It's too late to apologize to her but the least I can do is look that shame in the eye and acknowledge what I put her through."

The more he learned about his father the more he admired and feared him. He respected Roger for owning up to his actions and decisions that had caused Lucas's mother heartache and pain. But he worried that if he embraced the kind of relationship with his father that he yearned for, he'd end up hurt.

"I don't have the right to ask anything of you, Lucas. I know you're going to call the shots in our relationship as you should, but I care about you and I'd like us to be closer. However, if it never goes beyond an employer-employee relationship then I'll accept that and be grateful for it."

Lucas nodded. "There's no harm in taking things one day at a time."

Roger lifted his coffee mug in salute then they paid the bill and fetched their coats from their rooms before returning to the lobby.

"How does a person ever get used to this bitter cold?" Roger asked when they stopped by the door to button their jackets and put on their gloves.

"It grows on you," Lucas said, surprised at how easily the words came. "San Diego's mild climate definitely makes for an easier life." But at the end of the day it wasn't the weather you came home to—it was the people who loved you. Ava and Sophie popped into Lucas's head and he envisioned eating dinner with them and talking about their day. He didn't want to think about leaving Marietta and saying goodbye to them.

Ron opened the door and Lucas and his father approached. "Have a nice afternoon, gentlemen."

"Thank you, Ron."

Roger's hand bumped Ron's and Lucas saw his father give the bellman a ten-dollar tip.

"Thank you, sir!"

"That was nice of you," Lucas said. "Ron's saving money to take his wife to Hawaii in February."

"I've been to Hawaii once," Roger said. "Nice place."

"We'll take my rental car." Lucas pointed the key fob at the vehicle and unlocked the doors. Once they got inside and buckled up, he said, "The library is only a few blocks away."

"The courthouse is impressive." Roger peered out the window. "What's the population of the town?"

"Somewhere between ten and twelve thousand."

His father whistled between his teeth. "The teenagers must be bored out of their minds growing up in a place this small."

"I don't know," Lucas said, pulling into the lot behind the library. "Kids are the same everywhere whether they live in small towns or big cities. They hang out with their friends. In San Diego teens go to the beach and in Marietta they go skiing or sledding."

"Claire sent Brady and Seth to camps every summer and then we'd plan a family vacation before school started in August. We must have visited Disney World six times when they were little. I was tired of the place after the second visit."

Lucas turned off the motor and glanced across the seat. Roger stared in a trance out the windshield. "What's wrong?"

"I'm sorry."

"For what?" Lucas asked.

"For not thinking before I speak. I'm complaining about taking your half brothers to Disney World too often and I assume you've never been there."

"I spent my summer breaks in San Diego. Didn't go to any camps." Lucas blew out a breath. "This isn't going to work." He pointed at his father. "If you feel guilty for everything you say, you'll stop talking. If everything I tell you makes you feel bad, I'll stop talking. And we'll never get to know each other." He shoved his gloved hand through his hair. "I promised my mother before she died that I'd give you a chance."

Roger nodded then unbuckled his belt and they got out

of the car.

The library was crowded with women browsing bookshelves while kids sat in a circle inside the children's room and listened to a library worker read to them. Lucas went straight to the librarian's desk.

Dark eyes peered over the rim of her glasses. "May I help you, gentlemen?"

"I'm looking for a librarian named Kathleen Hardy."

"I'm sorry, Kathleen passed away several years ago. Is there something I can help you with?"

"I'd like to take care of a fine for my mother." Lucas felt his father's stare burning into him.

"Fines are usually paid online, but I'd be happy to help you." She typed on the keyboard. "What's your mother's name?"

"Carol Kendrick."

She entered the name then frowned. Typed it again. Then frowned again. "We don't have a card registered to a Carol Kendrick. Perhaps you have the wrong library?"

He shook his head. "This is the right library but it was a long time ago."

"Do you know the title of the overdue book?"

"*Can't You Sleep, Little Bear?*"

Her nails clicked against the keyboard then she leaned forward, her nose inches from the monitor. "Our records show that a copy of the book went missing in 1989."

"That would be the copy that's overdue."

"Carol Kendrick," she murmured. "Why does that name sound familiar?"

"I'm her son Lucas Kendrick."

The woman's eyes widened. "The Graff Hotel guest who was reported—"

"Missing during the last snowstorm."

"You went missing?" his father asked.

"It's a long story." Lucas nodded at the computer. "After my mother passed away, I found the book in her things. The inside cover had Marietta Library stamped on it." And between the pages had been a note signed by a Kathleen that said, *I think Lucas will love this one.* And the librarian had been right.

"Can you tell me the cost of replacing the book plus thirty years' worth of overdue fines?"

"The maximum fine is fifty dollars plus the price of the book, which is..." she peered at the computer "...seven dollars and ninety-nine cents."

"How much does the library charge per day for an overdue book?"

"Twenty cents per day."

Lucas glanced across the room. "Does the library keep a wish list of children's books?"

Her eyes sparkled. "Yes, we do." After a couple of clicks on the keyboard she said, "We have forty-six books on our fundraising list this year."

Lucas removed his checkbook from his back pocket and wrote out a draft for two thousand dollars. "I'd like to make this donation in my mother's name and ask that the money be used to pay for children's books."

Her smile widened after she read the amount of the

check. "This will more than cover the cost of all the books."

"Thank you," he said.

"Thank you, Mr. Kendrick."

He turned away but Roger grabbed his arm. "I'd like to match his donation and ask that the money also be used for the children's room."

"Oh, my," the librarian said. "The library board will be thrilled." She nodded. "Will this be in Carol Kendrick's name also?"

"No, this will be in Lucas Kendrick's name."

Lucas waited for his father to hand over the check then he thanked the librarian and they turned to leave.

"Wait." She went to the printer. "A receipt for your donation. Thank you so much, gentlemen."

Luck held the door open for his father. "What we just did will make the five o'clock news on KCMC radio."

"You're pulling my leg." Roger followed Lucas along the sidewalk.

"I wish I were."

"What's this about you getting lost in a snowstorm?"

Lucas unlocked the rental car. "It's a long story."

"I could use a drink." He grinned. "It's five o'clock somewhere."

Lucas laughed. "I haven't been to Grey's Saloon yet. It's a historic bar on Main Street."

"Let's check it out."

Lucas found a parking spot on the street a block away. A historical plaque by the door stated Ephraim Grey had established the bar in 1878.

Lucas thought he'd entered the Wild West when they stepped inside the bar. The plank floor popped and creaked beneath their shoes and he pictured cowboys and miners drinking in the saloon over a century ago. He and Roger claimed stools at the bar, which looked as old as the floors.

The barkeep slapped cocktail napkins down in front of them. "Reese Kendrick at your service."

"Roger Belfour and this is my son, Lucas Kendrick."

This was the first time Roger had introduced Lucas as *my son* and he was surprised that it felt...*okay*. Maybe even a little better than okay.

"What are the chances we're related?" The bartender grinned.

"Does anyone in your family hail from San Diego?" Lucas asked.

Reese shook his head. "It's probably better that I'm not connected to a city slicker. A cousin like you would tarnish my tough-guy image."

Lucas grinned. "You heard I got lost in the snowstorm."

Reese chuckled. "What can I get for you two?"

"He'll take a scotch on the rocks. I'll have a Dr Pepper," Lucas said.

"Comin' right up."

"You're going to make me drink alone?" Roger said.

"I want to be on my best behavior at dinner tonight."

"Why's that?"

"Because we're not dining alone."

"Oh?"

Reese returned with their drink order then set a bowl of

popcorn on the bar and left them alone.

"Claire posed a question the other day that I didn't have an answer for."

"What's that?"

"She asked if you planned on taking the Belfour name."

Lucas doubted those had been Claire's exact words. He suspected his stepmother had strongly objected to Lucas calling himself a Belfour.

"I haven't given it much thought," Lucas said.

"Good."

Lucas glanced at his father. "Good?"

"You should keep mother's surname." Roger nodded. "You're strong and proud like Carol. You've got integrity, which you didn't inherit from me." Roger sipped his drink. "And your last name won't affect your inheritance. You've been in my will for years."

"I don't expect—"

"I know you don't, but you're my son no matter what name you go by." He sipped his scotch. "Whom are we dining with?"

"Two beautiful ladies."

"Two?" Roger smiled.

Lucas grabbed a fistful of popcorn and shoved it into his mouth. "You want to hear the story about the snowstorm or not?"

"I'm all ears."

Lucas spent an hour entertaining his father with the details of that night, leaving out the part where he kissed Ava, instead focusing on the radio station's account and the nosy hotel staff.

"You can't make a move in this town without people hearing about it," Roger said. "I don't know that I could ever get used to that."

Lucas had been the kid who'd grown up with a single mother and no extended family and he liked the idea of people looking out for him, even if they were strangers.

"I need a nap," Roger said. "This cold air makes me tired."

Lucas signaled for the check. When his father reached for the tab, Lucas snatched it first. "I'm paying."

"I should pay since I crashed your vacation."

Lucas signed the slip then held up the company credit card. "You did pay."

His father laughed. "You have a sense of humor. I like that."

They stood and Reese hollered from the opposite end of the bar. "Don't get lost out there."

Lucas waved. As they walked back to the car, he glanced over his shoulder at the Copper Mountain Chic clothing boutique and remembered kissing Ava inside the industrial trash container behind the building. From here on out he'd always associate Dumpsters with kissing Ava.

Maybe you should keep that to yourself.

Chapter Twelve

"PROMISE ME YOU'LL be on your best behavior tonight."
Ava gathered her daughter's ponytail and twirled it
into a bun on top of her head then secured it with sparkly
hair clips. Sophie had asked if she could wear her princess
hairdo to the dinner at the hotel.

"Is Mr. Lucas's daddy nice?"

"I'm sure he is." Roger Belfour better not make a liar out
of Ava, because she'd spent the past two hours fielding
questions about a man she didn't have a high opinion of.

"What do you think?" She held a hand mirror behind
Sophie's head.

"Good." Sophie climbed down from the step stool.
"Thank you."

"You're welcome. Go put on your shiny shoes." Sophie
left the bathroom and Ava studied her reflection in the
mirror.

Tonight she'd curled her hair and the ringlets cascaded
over her shoulders and down the back of her long-sleeve
black cocktail dress. The outfit's neckline was modest but the
material hugged her curves in all the right places, making her
feel feminine and pretty. A strand of pink pearls matching
the teardrop pearl earrings added a pop of color. Her outfit

complimented Sophie's pink satin dress with a black bow around the waist.

She touched up the subtle pink lipstick then blotted her lips on a tissue. She wore more makeup tonight and wondered what Lucas would think of her smoky eyes. She'd known him nine days and they'd shared a few kisses but they'd never been on an official date. She hoped to make a good impression—not because she cared what Roger Belfour thought of her, but because tonight was important to Lucas.

When Lucas had told her that he was ready to give his father a chance, her heart had broken at the earnest light in his eyes. No matter how old a man grew, he still needed his father's acceptance and approval and she was awed by Lucas's courage. Time would tell if he and his father could find a path forward.

After one last look in the mirror she left the bathroom and fetched her and Sophie's dress coats from her bedroom closet. When she returned to the living room, her cell phone dinged with a text message. Lucas wanted to drive over and pick them up. She texted a thank you, saying they were already on their way. As much as she appreciated his offer, Ava preferred taking her car in case the evening ended in disaster and she needed to make a quick getaway.

"Hurry up, honey!"

Her daughter came out of her bedroom and Ava glanced at Sophie's shoes, making sure she had them on the correct feet, then helped her with her coat and mittens.

Ava grabbed her evening clutch and they left the apartment. She held tight to her daughter's hand as they carefully descended the fire escape. When they made it to the car, Ava adjusted the strap on Sophie's booster seat then she started the engine and turned on the heat. "My legs are freezing."

"And my toes," Sophie said.

The drive to the hotel took five minutes and on a Tuesday night the parking lot wasn't crowded. Ron opened the lobby door for them and grinned. "You ladies look lovely."

"Thank you, Ron."

"May I take your jackets and put them in the coatroom?" he asked.

Ava handed over her coat and helped Sophie off with hers. "Thank you."

His eyes twinkled. "They're waiting in the dining room."

Ava grabbed Ron's arm when he made a move to step past her. "Is he…?" She quirked an eyebrow.

"Mr. Belfour?"

Ava nodded.

"He's been quite pleasant during his stay."

Pleasant could mean anything from nice to arrogant. After Ron walked off, Ava took a deep breath hoping to still the butterflies in her stomach. She grasped Sophie's hand and they walked the short distance to the restaurant. They paused in the doorway, her gaze skimming the room. The men were seated at a table by the windows. Lucas must have sensed her stare, because he glanced her way—his eyes widening when he spotted her.

Her face warmed at Lucas's appreciative stare and both men stood when she and Sophie reached the table.

"Ava." Lucas kissed her cheek. "You look stunning."

Then he crouched down and said, "Princess Sophie, you're as pretty as your mother tonight."

Instead of saying thank you as she'd been coached, Sophie hugged Lucas and Ava caught the surprised look on Roger's face when Lucas returned her daughter's hug.

"Roger," Lucas said. "I'd like you to meet Ava Moore and her little girl, Sophie."

"It's a pleasure meeting you, ladies," Roger said.

Lucas held out a chair for Ava, but Sophie stepped past her mother and said, "I'm gonna sit by Mr. Lucas."

"Whatever you want, Princess Sophie." Lucas helped Sophie onto the seat of the chair and Roger pulled out Ava's chair for her.

"Thank you," she murmured.

Before any pleasantries were exchanged the waiter appeared. "Would you like me to bring the wine, sir?"

Lucas looked at Ava. "I ordered a bottle of wine for the table, but if you'd like something else?"

"Wine is fine."

The waiter departed.

Sophie tugged on Lucas's suit jacket sleeve and pointed a tiny finger at Roger. "Is he your daddy?"

"Indeed I am, Sophie." Roger smiled. "You can call me Mr. Roger if you'd like. Or Mr. Old Man."

Sophie giggled then looked at Lucas. "He's funny."

Roger nodded to Ava. "Lucas tells me you recently moved to Marietta to be closer to your mother-in-law."

"I'm still getting used to the long winters," Ava said.

The waiter appeared with a wine bottle in one hand and

sparkling apple cider in the other. "Would you like cider, miss?"

"I thought Sophie would enjoy sharing a toast with us," Lucas said.

"Sure." Ava appreciated his thoughtfulness.

The waiter filled Sophie's glass with bubbly cider then poured wine for the adults. "The hors d'oeuvres will be out shortly, sir."

"A toast." Lucas raised his wineglass.

Sophie copied the adults.

"To the most beautiful princesses in the kingdom of Marietta and to new beginnings," he said.

"Hear, hear," Roger echoed.

They clanged their glasses together and Ava was surprised when Roger leaned across the table to tap his glass against Sophie's. He wasn't acting like a man who'd abandoned one of his children.

Sophie crinkled her nose after she sipped the drink.

"What's the matter, princess?" Lucas asked. "You don't like it?"

"It tickles my nose," she said, and everyone laughed.

"Despite the bone-chilling temperatures," Roger said, "Marietta is charming." He waved his hand at the room. "I'm impressed with the Graff. I wasn't expecting a gem like this in a small town."

"Bob gave Roger the rundown on the hotel's history when he checked in," Lucas said.

"Has Lucas given you the five-cent tour yet?" Ava spoke to Roger.

"We visited the library earlier today," Roger said.

"Mommy takes me to the library," Sophie said. "I like to look at the princess books."

Lucas moved Sophie's glass away from the edge of the table. For a man who'd never had children he instinctively knew what to keep an eye on. "I wanted to pay my mother's fine," he said.

"He did more than pay Carol's overdue-book fine. He gave a generous donation in his mother's name to the children's section."

"Roger also gave a donation," Lucas said. "Then we stopped by Grey's Saloon."

Roger chuckled. "And Lucas met a long-lost relative."

"Relative?" Ava glanced between the men.

"Reese Kendrick," Lucas said. "The bartender. And we're not related, which Reese is happy about since he also heard I'd been lost in the snowstorm."

Ava smiled. "Did you tell your fa—Roger about that?" She hoped he'd left out the part where he'd spent the night at her apartment.

"I did."

The waiter arrived at the table with the appetizers. "The lobster-stuffed mushrooms, sir, and the baguettes with Nutella."

Ava's eyes burned as she stared at the mini heart-shaped pieces of toasted bread slathered with Sophie's favorite spread. She blinked hard until the urge to cry passed.

Sophie pointed to the bread. "Look, Mr. Lucas." Her eyes widened.

Lucas leaned over and whispered, "I told them I was eating with a princess tonight."

"Can I have one?" she asked Lucas and he looked at Ava.

"Of course," Ava said.

Lucas set a piece of heart-shaped bread on Sophie's plate and by the way her daughter smiled at him one would believe he'd just slid a pair of glass slippers on her feet.

After Sophie took a bite she looked across the table and said, "Mr. Roger, do you want one of my hearts?"

"Honey, I don't think—"

"I would love one," Roger said.

Ava couldn't tell if Roger was putting on a show for her or if he genuinely enjoyed her daughter's company.

"Thank you," Roger said, helping himself to a chocolate-covered piece of bread. He took a bite then his eyes widened and he moaned loudly. Sophie giggled and looked at Lucas. "I think your daddy likes it."

Ava swallowed a gulp of wine. She was beginning to understand why Lucas wanted to give Roger a chance.

"Ava?" Lucas held up the platter of stuffed mushrooms and she put two on her plate.

The conversation shifted back to Marietta. Roger asked questions about the Copper Mountain ski resort and Ava recommended he drive into the mountains while he was in town. "Have you taken Roger by Copper Mountain Chocolate yet?"

"Mr. Lucas bought me chocolate Christmas trees with sprinkles there," Sophie told Roger.

The waiter stopped by the table and asked if they were

ready to order. He looked at Ava first. After working at the hotel for two years she knew the menu by heart. "I'll have the grilled salmon, please."

"For you, miss?"

Sophie stared at her mother and Ava asked, "Would you like chicken fingers and fries?"

Sophie nodded.

"Very well, miss." His gaze shifted to Roger.

"Rib eye steak, medium well. Baked potato. No salad." Roger closed his menu.

"And for you, sir?" The waiter turned to Lucas.

"I'll also have the rib eye medium well, baked potato and no salad."

The waiter collected the menus. "Another bottle of wine, perhaps?"

Ava placed her hand over the top of her glass. "I'm fine, thank you."

"No thanks," Lucas said.

After the waiter disappeared, Roger spoke to Ava. "Lucas tells me that you're putting your business degree to work forming a co-op."

"I'm teaming up with a group of very determined women."

"Ava's business partners are single mothers," Lucas said.

She was relieved Lucas hadn't brought up Stan Mueller or mentioned that he was competing with Ava for the same property.

"I'd like to hear more about the co-op," Roger said.

"The plan is to open a store that sells refurbished vintage

furniture and home décor. The profits will be used to help the women defray the cost of furthering their education."

"Wouldn't single mothers be eligible for education assistance?" Roger asked.

"In some cases they are," Ava said. "But scholarships only cover the cost of classes. Single moms have trouble paying for textbooks, computers, and childcare while they're in class."

"Ava's business plan includes free childcare for the co-op members," Lucas said.

"We're partnering with the high school community service clubs and have a list of young girls and a few boys who will watch the kids."

"Where did you find your investors?" Roger asked.

"Actually we don't have any investors. When my husband passed away I received a bereavement settlement from the military, which I've used to purchase the inventory." Right now the furniture and items were being stored in the basement of a church in town.

"You have a degree," Roger said. "What do you get out of this co-op?"

"The satisfaction of helping single mothers achieve their dreams." Ava smiled. "All mothers want their children to succeed and good-paying jobs will help them provide more opportunities for their kids."

Roger glanced across the table. "Lucas was blessed with a strong mother."

"Mr. Lucas."

"Yes, Sophie?"

While her daughter regaled Lucas with the story of the

hunt for the lost mitten at preschool earlier that day, Ava's thoughts turned inward. After everything Lucas had told her about his upbringing and the tough times Carol struggled through while raising him alone, Ava had wanted to dislike Roger Belfour. But witnessing the men converse and seeing how comfortable Lucas appeared with his father, she sensed they both desired a true reconciliation. She'd been fortunate to experience a wonderful relationship with her father as well as her foster father. She wished for Lucas to have those memories, too.

Any thoughts she'd harbored about Roger showing up in Marietta with an ulterior motive were put to rest when she recognized the genuine affection and respect in the older man's eyes as he listened to his son speak. Lucas may have been born in Marietta but his destiny was in San Diego working at Belfour Investments with his father.

Ava's heart hurt—not for Lucas, but for her and Sophie. When she was with Lucas, everything in her crazy world made sense and she'd begun to believe he was a real-life prince. But the dream of the three of them becoming a family was shriveling up right before her eyes.

"Mr. Roger," Sophie said.

"Yes, young lady?"

"Do you have a princess?"

Roger glanced between Ava and Lucas, his mouth twitching. "I don't have a princess waiting for me at home, I have a queen."

Sophie's mouth dropped open. "You have a queen?"

"I'm afraid my queen can be quite fussy."

Sophie shook her head. "Princesses are nice." Sophie looked at Lucas. "I'm a nice princess, right, Mr. Lucas?"

Lucas stared at Ava. "You and your mother are very nice and very pretty princesses."

Their waiter arrived with dinner and Roger regaled Sophie with stories of his childhood and all the trouble he'd gotten into as a young boy. A half-hour later, the staff cleared the table and their waiter offered a dessert menu. Ava and Lucas declined but Roger agreed to share a piece of chocolate silk pie with Sophie, drawing the evening out longer.

As soon as her daughter finished her pie, Ava spoke. "It's getting late. Sophie and I should be on our way." She smiled at Lucas's father. "It was a pleasure meeting you, Roger. Thank you for dinner."

"The pleasure was all mine, Ava. I hope we'll see each other again before I depart."

"When are you leaving?" she asked.

"Thursday."

Lucas helped Sophie down from her chair and her daughter walked over to Roger and hugged him. The shocked expression on the older man's face was almost comical. "Bye, Mr. Roger."

"Goodbye, Princess Sophie. I hope to have the pleasure of seeing you again in the near future."

"Maybe I can come to your house and play."

"I hope you do." Roger smiled at Ava. "She's as charming as her mother."

"I'll walk you to your car." Lucas looked at Roger. "Be back shortly."

Ava took several steps toward the exit but stopped when she noticed Sophie wasn't following. She checked over her shoulder and caught her daughter sliding her hand into Lucas's.

One of the waiters must have signaled Ron that they were leaving, because he waited by door with their coats. Ron helped Ava on with hers and Lucas helped Sophie.

Ron opened the door and Lucas accompanied them across the parking lot. When they reached the Toyota, Ava unlocked the car and helped Sophie into the booster seat. After she slid behind the wheel, Lucas leaned his head inside the car. "Goodnight, princess. Don't let the bedbugs bite."

Sophie giggled. "I wish you were my daddy, Mr. Lucas."

Ava started the car and Lucas closed the back door.

"Thank you for the lovely dinner," she said. "I enjoyed meeting your father."

He leaned down to kiss her, but she turned her head and his lips grazed her cheek. "Drive safe." He closed the door.

Thankful he hadn't mentioned her meeting with Sandra earlier in the day, Ava backed out of the spot. When she checked her side mirror before pulling into the street, Lucas was still standing in the lot staring after her.

LUCAS STARED INTO space long after the Toyota left the hotel parking lot. Ava had dodged his kiss and he didn't know why. He went over the evening in his head, fast-forwarding and rewinding, but he couldn't pinpoint a word or a facial expression that signaled she'd been upset.

Shoot. He'd forgotten to ask how her meeting with Sandra had gone that morning. Maybe Sandra had given her bad news and that's why Ava hadn't mentioned it when Roger had asked about the co-op.

The wind picked up and cold air seeped through his sport coat so he headed inside. Ron opened the lobby door when Lucas reached the entrance.

"Thank you."

"You're welcome, sir."

Lucas studied the doorman. "I can ask you a hundred times to call me Lucas, but you won't, will you?"

"No, sir."

"Would you call me Lucas if we passed each other walking down Main Street?"

"Yes, sir."

Lucas nodded. "Good." He returned to the dining room and joined his father at the table.

"Ava's a lovely woman, Lucas. And that little Sophie is a pip."

"We met on New Year's Eve." Lucas studied Roger. "Do you believe in love at first sight?"

"I do, and I also believe very few people ever experience it."

"Why?"

"A love like that takes a leap of faith. People want proof that something exists." Roger waved his hand. "If true love came along a person might miss the signals because they weren't looking for it."

"If you had the chance to go back and live your life over again would you still marry Claire?"

Roger nodded. "A woman like Claire is my destiny. To marry for true love I'd have to be a different person. Money and success is important to me. At least it was until recently."

"What do you mean?"

"I've always possessed a big ego. Being prosperous has been a top priority for me until you came back into my life and opened my eyes." He pushed his coffee cup away. "Through the years I've watched you grow into a confident, successful young man and it's a blow to my pride that I had nothing to do with the way you turned out."

"Why didn't you contact me after my mother died?"

"I thought about it." Roger stared into space. "Often."

"But...?"

"I was a coward. Even though I'd rejected you, I didn't want you to do the same to me."

Wow. Lucas hadn't seen that coming.

"I did Carol wrong and I did you wrong, Lucas. It was a wake-up call for me when Claire had her hissy fit after the Christmas party and I didn't stand up for you." He shifted in his seat. "After you left town I came to the conclusion that if I wanted a relationship with you *I* would need to change. I couldn't be the same man I was before you reached out to me." He smiled. "I told Claire that if she couldn't accept you were my son and treat you with respect then it was time to end our marriage."

Lucas was shocked. "It's never been my intention to break up your marriage."

"Of course you didn't," he said. "Claire had been holding my mistake with your mother over my head for decades. I'm fifty-nine years old and I've made a lot of bad choices in my life. I don't want to make another one. I warned Claire that you were part of the family and her behavior toward you had better change if she wanted us to remain married."

The purpose of Lucas trying to make the deal with Stan Mueller was to solidify his position in his father's family, but after Roger's impassioned speech Lucas realized he'd already been accepted into the fold.

"Claire accused me at the Christmas party of trying to sabotage your company," Lucas said.

"Claire says a lot of things that are nonsense. I don't ever want you to feel as if you need to prove yourself to me. I'm the one who has something to prove to you."

If his father had the courage to speak the truth then Lucas needed to also. "A while back I contacted an alumni from the business school at ASU. Stan Mueller. He's—"

"I know who he is."

Lucas explained everything even the fact that was competing against Ava for the building.

"No matter what happens, you and I should discuss expanding Belfour Investments into other avenues like historical properties," Roger said. "I'm glad you told me about Mueller, because I've been waiting for the right moment to talk to you about something."

"What's that?"

"I'd like you to be a partner in the company, Lucas."

Partner? "What about Seth and Brady?"

"When I tell them they can quit working for me, they'll be ecstatic and I'm sure they'll thank you for accepting my offer."

Lucas's throat tightened at the respect shining in Roger's eyes.

"There's no one I'd rather have with me at the helm of Belfour Investments than you, Lucas." Roger signaled the waiter for the check. "Think about my offer. It would mean more travel for you and longer hours." Roger handed his credit card to the waiter.

"I'll consider it," Lucas said.

"Good. Now about that older woman who helped Carol when she arrived in town."

"Mable Bramble?"

"I'd like to pay her a visit tomorrow."

Nothing like starting off hump day with a bang.

Chapter Thirteen

WEDNESDAY BEFORE NOON Lucas returned to the hotel after talking with Sandra Reynolds. He'd texted Roger to meet him in the lobby, but his father wasn't there when Lucas entered the hotel.

"Mr. Belfour is in the bar, sir," Ron said.

Jeez. Maybe Roger was worried about meeting Mable Bramble and needed a shot of scotch for courage. Lucas headed toward the lounge but stopped short when his father walked out of the bar. "What's that?" he pointed to the liquor bottle in Roger's hand.

"Peppermint schnapps. I can't very well show up without a gift."

"I don't know if Mable drinks," Lucas said.

"If she's as crusty as you say, then she drinks." They left the lobby and got into the rental car. "How was your talk with Ms. Reynolds?" Roger asked.

"It fell through." Lucas hadn't been surprised when Sandra had broken the news to him that she was partnering with Ava's co-op. He'd figured that was why Ava hadn't brought up her meeting with Sandra at dinner last night. On the way back to the hotel Lucas had phoned Ava to congratulate her but his call had gone straight to voice-mail, so he'd left a message asking her to contact him.

"There'll be other deals," Roger said.

Lucas left the hotel lot and drove across town. When he parked in front of the Bramble House B&B, he asked, "Are you sure you want to meet Mable? She's pushing ninety, but she's not afraid to speak her mind."

"I'm going to get a tongue-lashing, aren't I?"

His father would be lucky if insults were the only thing the old woman hurled at him. They left the car and climbed the porch steps.

Roger rang the bell.

The door opened immediately and they came face-to-face with the old woman. Lucas sent his father an I-told-you-so look. "Good afternoon, Mable."

She reached for the eyeglasses hanging on the chain around her neck and slid them on then squinted at Roger. "I wondered if you'd bring this scoundrel by."

"Mable, this is my father, Roger Belfour."

"It's a pleasure to meet you, Mable," Roger said.

"You, sir, may call me madam."

Lucas expected her to invite them into the house but when she didn't, he said, "Roger would like a word with you."

After several long seconds, she waved them into the foyer.

"You have a beautiful home, madam." Roger held out the liquor bottle. "A little peppermint schnapps for you."

Mable stared daggers at the bottle and Lucas thought she might refuse the gift but after a moment she accepted the peace offering. "I like a little schnapps in my hot chocolate." Her gaze swung to Lucas. "Don't tell my niece. She believes I'm a teetotaler." She glanced between the men. "Is this going to require coffee?"

"I'd love a cup, thank you," Roger said.

She pointed to the coat stand in the corner. "Take off your jackets." She left them in the hall and went into the dining room.

Roger winked. "I like her."

When they entered the other room, Lucas caught Mable hiding the bottle of schnapps in the back of a cabinet. She closed the door and then poured three cups of coffee. After she sat at the table, Lucas and his father took their seats.

Roger cleared his throat. "Madam—"

Mable held up a hand. "I don't want to hear excuses for your reprehensible behavior toward Carol. Back in the day we called men like you worthless bounders."

His father didn't flinch, but Lucas squirmed in his chair.

"I found Carol sitting at the bus stop in November wearing only a light-weight jacket," Mable said. "Her eyes were hollow and her lips were blue from the cold." The dragon lady's nostrils flared as she gained steam. "In spite of her circumstances Carol proved to be a strong young lady. And she took excellent care of Lucas." Mable shook a knobby finger. "Not for one moment do I believe your son would have been better off with you." The finger swung to Lucas. "The sincere, honorable and respectful young man you are today is because of your mother." The finger returned to Roger. "Not because of you."

"I agree," Roger said. "Carol did a fine job raising Lucas."

"What is it you have to say?" she asked.

"Thank you," Roger said.

Mable's head snapped back.

"As one of the matriarchs of this fine town I wish to express my gratitude for the compassion you showed Carol. Lucas tells me you helped her get into an apartment and made sure she had a home to go to when she and Lucas were released from the hospital."

"Carol was the one who worked hard to keep a roof over her head and take care of Lucas."

"I've learned to never underestimate a woman's determination," Roger said.

"Maybe there's hope for you yet."

Lucas hid a smile behind his coffee mug.

"How do you plan to make this up to your son?" she asked.

"I will never be able to compensate Lucas for abandoning him and his mother. I can only hope that with time he'll will forgive me." Roger didn't flinch beneath the old woman's gaze. "My appreciation for how you helped Carol and my son is sincere and heartfelt. They were fortunate to have you in their lives for a short while."

Mable nodded. "What happens with you two now?"

"Lucas and I will be running Belfour Investments together," Roger said.

"In San Diego?"

Lucas nodded.

"That's too bad." Mable dropped her gaze. "Marietta needs more young people settling here."

"I'll be back to visit," Lucas said.

Mable straightened in her chair. "Oh?"

Lucas smiled. "Marietta feels like home, Mable."

"As it should, young man."

Roger cleared his throat. "I would be grateful if you'd look out for Lucas when he does visit."

Mable frowned. "What do you mean?"

"My son needs a grandmother."

Her cheeks turned pink.

"*I* don't have the right to ask this, madam, but I'm soliciting you on Carol's behalf."

Mable's eyelashes fluttered like hummingbird wings.

Oh, brother. Roger was laying it on thick. "I'd be honored to call you Grandma," Lucas said.

Mable's eyebrows crawled up her forehead. "You may call me Grandmother, young man."

"We've taken up enough of your time, madam." Roger pushed his chair back.

Mable followed them to the front door and waited while they put their coats and gloves on. Lucas grasped Mable's hands and whispered in her ear. "Homemade chocolate chip cookies are my favorite." He kissed her cheek then went outside, allowing Roger a moment alone with Mable.

Lucas breathed in a lungful of cold air and closed his eyes. When he returned to San Diego he'd buy his snooty *grandma* a gaudy souvenir—maybe a piece of glass with a colored jellyfish inside it. What fun was having a grandmother if you couldn't tease her?

The door opened and Roger joined him on the porch. "I like Mable. She's got gumption."

Lucas smiled when he thought of another woman in Marietta who had gumption—Ava. Then his smile faded when he realized he'd have to say goodbye to her and Princess Sophie.

"Thanks for taking the time to meet this morning." Ava walked Phil Hutchinson to the door in the back room of the dress shop. They'd spent the past two hours discussing renovations for the co-op.

"I think what you're doing is really great, Ava, and I'll make sure the work is done right." Phil opened the door and almost plowed into Lucas. "Sorry about that." He stepped past Lucas. "I'll see you tomorrow, Ava."

A rush of chilly air followed Lucas and Roger inside.

Ava forced a smile. "What a nice surprise." She wished Lucas had come alone so they could talk in private about Sandra's decision to partner with the co-op.

"I tried to get a hold of you earlier," Lucas said.

"Phil and I were discussing the renovations for the co-op."

"Congratulations." Lucas's smile reached his eyes. "I'm excited for you and the other women."

"I'll add my congratulations too," Roger said. "I hope your co-op is a huge success."

"Thank you. I'm very excited."

"Ava—" Sandra stopped in the doorway when she saw Lucas and Roger. "I'm sorry," she said. "I thought you were alone."

"Sandra, this is Roger Belfour, Lucas's father," Ava said.

Roger offered his hand. "It's a pleasure to meet you, Ms. Reynolds."

"Please call me Sandra."

"I apologize for barging in," Roger said, "but I asked Lucas to bring me by so I could see your building."

"I'd be happy to give you a tour," Sandra said.

Roger nodded to his son. "I've offered Lucas a partnership in my company and I think he's on to something with these historic properties. If you have the time I'd enjoy hearing your reasons for buying this building."

"Of course," Sandra said. "Take your coat off and we'll chat in the store." After Roger hung up his jacket, he followed Sandra into the dress shop.

Left alone in the back room with Lucas, Ava smiled. "Partner? That's fantastic. Congratulations." Last night she'd been prepared to dislike Roger for abandoning Lucas, but had been caught off guard by how much she'd liked him. She'd noticed the yearning in the older man's eyes when he looked at his son and unless he was a consummate liar, Roger deeply regretted the pain his actions had caused Lucas and his mother.

"Thanks." Lucas's expression sobered. "Roger's offer took me by surprise."

"It sounds like he wants to make up for lost time."

Lucas's gaze darted past Ava. "Everything is happening so fast."

Ava grasped his hand. "What's really bothering you?"

"If I accept the partnership then my father will think I've moved on from the past." He pulled his hand free and paced in front of Ava. "I feel like I'm skipping a bunch of steps in this reconciliation process. I'm happy that I've earned Roger's respect but it's going to take longer for me to learn to trust him."

"The process will play itself out whether you're an employee or partner. My father used to say 'go big or don't go at all'."

He caressed her cheek. "I'm really happy the co-op is becoming a reality."

"What happens with Stan Mueller?" she asked.

"He moved on."

"I'm sorry."

Lucas brushed a strand of hair away from her face, his finger lingering against her skin. "There will be other opportunities now that I'm a partner in Roger's company."

"I guess we both got what we wanted." If that was true, then why did she feel empty inside?

The bells on the front door jingled. "That's Tilly and Sophie," Ava said, unable to tear her gaze away from Lucas's face.

"Hi, Mr. Roger." Sophie's voice rang out. "Are you gonna buy your queen one of Aunt Sandra's dresses?"

Roger laughed. "Not today, Princess Sophie."

Ava walked over to the doorway and spied on Lucas's

father and her daughter.

Roger pointed to her head. "That's a beautiful crown you're wearing."

"Mr. Lucas gave it to me when he ate spaghetti and slept on Mommy's couch."

Time to intervene before her daughter said too much.

"Mr. Lucas says I'm the prettiest princess in the Marietta kingdom."

"You are the prettiest, princess," Lucas said, trailing Ava into the dress shop.

"Mr. Lucas!" Sophie ran toward Lucas and he scooped her up into his arms. "I wore my princess crown," she said.

Lucas nodded to his father. "Princess Sophie and her mother live in the castle tower upstairs." Then he said, "I'd like you to meet Ava's mother-in-law, Tilly Moore. Tilly, my father, Roger Belfour."

After Roger and Tilly exchanged pleasantries, Roger walked over to the display window and sniffed the air. "I smell cigar smoke."

Sandra joined Roger. "It's faint, but I smell it, too." She pointed to the window. "I think it's the chair."

"It is," Tilly said. Everyone stared at Ava's mother-in-law. "The chair belonged to Albert Graff."

"Who's this Albert chap?" Roger asked.

"He built the Graff Hotel," Sandra said.

Ava joined the discussion. "When the chair was stored in the hotel attic, Angelica said she smelled cigar smoke whenever she went up there."

"Albert sat in that chair and smoked his cigars in the hotel lobby," Tilly said.

"What happened to the man?" Roger asked.

"He contracted tuberculosis and sold the hotel in 1904," Sandra said. "He spent time at the famous Cragmor in Colorado Springs." Sandra ran her hand over the back of the chair. "According to a newspaper interview Albert intended to return to the Graff after he was cured, but he ended up passing away at Cragmor."

"He's back," Tilly said. "And he'd prefer to sit in the hotel lobby instead of that window."

Roger cleared his throat. "That's quite a story."

Ava didn't know what to think, but it was time to end the conversation before Tilly began talking out loud to Albert Graff. "I need to get back to work," she said. "Tilly, will you take Sophie into the back room? I'd like your opinion on something."

Lucas set Sophie on her feet and Tilly followed her. "Roger, it was a pleasure meeting you. I hope you'll return to Marietta and visit us again sometime."

"I would love to see Montana in the summer," he said.

"When are you leaving town?" Sandra asked.

"Tomorrow." Roger smiled at Lucas. "My son and I have many business decisions to make in the coming months."

Ava forced a brave smile even though her heart was shattering in her chest. "Then I guess this is goodbye." If she didn't get away from Lucas right then she'd start bawling. She stepped forward and hugged him, inhaling his scent, memorizing the feel of his arms around her. "Have a safe flight back to San Diego."

"Ava, I—"

She shook her head. If he said one more word she'd beg him not to leave. She hurried into the back room. "I forgot something upstairs." Ava took the keys from her purse. "Be right back." She stepped into the alley then hurried up the fire escape and into her apartment. As soon as she closed the door, she sank to the floor and bawled like a baby.

※※※≪≪≪

"IT'S FRIDAY NIGHT." Roger stopped in the doorway of Lucas's office. "You've been working late all week."

Lucas had been working extra late every night since he'd returned to San Diego twenty-right days ago. "I need to finish this proposal."

"Mind if I sit?" Roger didn't wait for an invite. He pulled out the chair across from the desk and made himself comfortable. "Claire asked if you were coming to the barbecue on Sunday."

"Sure." Lucas scribbled a note, reminding himself to double-check his figures before signing off on the proposal.

Roger released a loud sigh. "If you won't say it, I will."

"What's that?"

"You made the wrong choice."

Lucas glanced up. "What are you taking about?"

"You chose me over Ava."

"Have you been drinking?" His father kept a liquor cart in his office for when he met with clients.

"No, I haven't been drinking."

Lucas checked the clock above the door. "Isn't Claire expecting you home soon?"

"Put the pen down and listen to me."

Startled by Roger's stern tone, Lucas gave his father his undivided attention.

"I've dreamed of having a relationship with you for thirty years. That you were willing to give me a chance when I didn't deserve one speaks volumes about your character. Every day I look forward to coming into the office and working with you." Roger studied his hands.

"Are you firing me?"

"No, but this arrangement is all one-sided—my side."

"Did I do something to upset Claire?" Actually Lucas believed things had been better between him and his father's wife.

"This has nothing to do with Claire."

"Are Seth and Brady angry about something?"

Roger shook his head. "Brady is thrilled with his new job at the shipyard and Seth couldn't be happier working as an artist in residence in San Ysidro."

"If everyone is happy—"

"You're not happy." Roger's expression sobered. "You stay past eight every night and I've seen your car in the parking lot on weekends."

He'd rather be at work than sit in his empty apartment thinking about Ava and Sophie.

"I haven't been a part of your life for decades and you have every right to tell me to mind my own business, but I believe you're miserable because you're in love with Ava

Moore and you miss Princess Sophie."

Lucas had known Ava and her daughter less than two weeks before he'd left Marietta, but the pair had stolen his heart. "You don't have to worry about me quitting and leaving you in a bind."

Roger's head jerked as if Lucas had slapped him. "The thought never crossed my mind."

"I'm sorry." Lucas rubbed the knot at the back of his neck. "I've been stressed out over this proposal."

"No, you haven't." Roger shook his head. "The proposal is fine. You're stressed out because you don't know how to tell me you're unhappy." Roger held up a hand. "I'm not kicking you out of the company, I'm kicking you out of the office."

"What do you mean?"

"I want you to keep working for Belfour Investments but you're going to do so in Marietta."

"Our clients are in San Diego."

Roger shrugged. "So you fly into the office once a month for a few days of back-to-back meetings. The rest of the time all you need is a phone and your computer."

"But—"

"Son, I've done nothing for you all these years. As your father I want to know what it feels like to help you. Go make a life with Ava and Sophie."

"You and I just reconciled."

"That's not going to change, Lucas. I won't let it. We'll talk on the phone regularly and it doesn't always have to be about business. We'll see each other for a few days a month when you fly in for meetings." Roger smiled. "Maybe you could bring Ava and Sophie with you. I'd love to take Sophie to the San Diego Zoo."

Lucas was humbled by Roger's offer. "I haven't spoken to Ava since we left. What if she doesn't feel the same about me?"

"You won't know unless you ask her." Roger grinned. "I spoke to Tilly the other day. The grand opening of the co-op is the second Saturday of February."

"Next weekend?"

Roger stood. "No matter what you decide about Ava, you should attend the opening."

"Why's that?"

"Ava named the co-op Carol's Closet." Roger left, closing the door behind him.

Lucas got up from his desk and stood in front of the window overlooking San Diego's central business district. He'd felt an immediate connection with Ava at the New Year's Eve ball. She'd also felt the attraction otherwise she wouldn't have returned his kiss. Each time they'd been together following that night Ava had stolen a little piece of his heart.

Like his mother Ava was a strong, loving single mom trying to make a good life for her daughter. But that's where the similarities ended. Carol Kendrick had never gotten involved in the community. She'd focused on her job and raising her son. When Lucas had left the nest, his mom had spent her free time reading, watching TV or resting.

But Ava—sweet, beautiful Ava—was a devoted working

mother, looked after her mother-in-law, and still found time to give back to her community. Life hadn't been easy for either woman, but unlike Lucas's mom, who couldn't let go of the past and those who'd hurt her, Ava hadn't let the past define her, and she continued moving forward toward a better future for herself and Sophie.

A future Lucas wanted to be a part of.

Chapter Fourteen

AVA STARED AT her reflection in the bathroom mirror. The last time she'd dolled herself up had been the night she had dinner with Lucas and his father at the hotel—back in early January. She'd planned to wear the same outfit for the grand opening of Carol's Closet this afternoon but yesterday Sandra had gifted her a dress from the shop, insisting Ava wear it today. The buttercream lace sheath with long sleeves and a rounded neckline made her feel feminine and pretty. She turned her head to the right then to the left, satisfied she looked businesslike with her hair pinned up.

"Are you ready, Sophie?" The party kicked off in less than an hour.

"I'm coming!" Her daughter's voice carried through the apartment.

Ava turned off the light and left the bathroom. This day…this dream had been in the works a long time and she should be over-the-moon excited. Instead, she'd woken in morning with a heavy heart because Lucas wasn't here to share this moment with her.

The Moore ladies had been in a funk since Lucas had left town with Roger. Ava believed Sophie's grumpy moods were the result of missing Lucas, so she and Tilly had joined forces to keep Sophie as busy as possible, but their efforts helped only so much. At night when Ava tucked her daughter into bed, Sophie would ask when Lucas was coming to visit them again.

More times than she could count Ava had picked up the phone to call Lucas and just say *hi* but she'd chickened out, afraid she'd confess that she was in love with him. At night when she lay in her bed alone she called herself every kind of fool for not revealing her feelings before he left town. If she hadn't had Sophie to consider, Ava would have taken a leap of faith and put her heart on the line, but her life was in Marietta and Lucas's was in San Diego. A long-distance relationship would only lead to heartache.

"I can't find my shoes." Sophie stood in the bedroom doorway in a blue frilly dress and white tights. Earlier Ava had put her daughter's hair in pigtails and tied blue-and-white ribbons around them.

"I see you're wearing your princess crown again." Heaven help Ava if the crown Lucas had given Sophie ever broke. "Your white shoes are in your closet in a pink box."

The back door opened and Tilly entered the apartment, wearing a dress and nylons. "You look pretty, Tilly." Ava narrowed her eyes. "There's something different about your hair."

"I colored it."

The orange curls had been toned down with brown highlights. "I like it. You look very sophisticated." Tilly rolled her eyes and Ava laughed.

"I peeked into the dress shop before I came up. The

judge brought Mable Bramble with him and his neighbor Gladys. Oh, and all the ladies in the co-op are downstairs, too."

Ava had checked on things a short while ago before coming up to the apartment to change her clothes. Three girls from the high school were in charge of the childcare room so the mothers in the co-op could enjoy the party without worrying about their kids getting into trouble. Sandra had suggested they give out door prizes and she'd donated gift cards from the dress shop. Ava had selected a few vintage décor items from the co-op and Sage Carrigan had donated gift-wrapped boxes of treats from the Copper Mountain Chocolate shop.

"Don't you look pretty, Sophie," Tilly said when her granddaughter joined them.

They left the apartment and walked through the alley and around to the front door of the dress shop. Ava spotted Sandra and Mable Bramble chatting with Angelica and her daughter, Elena. Three of Ava's co-workers from the hotel had shown up on their day off to help Ava celebrate. Tilly and Sophie went to say hello to the ladies.

The judge pulled Ava aside. "I want to thank you," he said.

"For what?"

"For accepting Sandra's offer to manage the dress shop, so she's free to travel with me."

"I'm grateful for this opportunity, Alistair." Ava had turned in her two weeks' notice at the Graff the day after Lucas left town. At the end of January she'd taken over the dress shop full-time when the judge and Sandra had left for Australia. "Where are you two flying off to next?"

"Medjumbe Island, Mozambique. It's an all-inclusive resort." He pressed a finger to his lips. "Don't mention anything to Sandra. I haven't told her yet."

"That sounds lovely." She glanced across the room. "I better mingle for a bit." Ava introduced the ladies in the co-op to members of the business community and offered tours of the back room, the workshop in the basement and the daycare. An hour after the opening, Sandra suggested Ava give her speech.

She walked over to the display window and waited for the group to quiet down. She and Sandra had agreed that Albert Graff's chair should be returned to the hotel. It now sat in the lobby facing the door and every once in a while one of the hotel employees or a guest would report smelling a cigar odor in the lobby.

Ava clapped her hands. "May I have your attention please?" She smiled at the faces gathered in front of her. "I'd like to thank Sandra Reynolds for partnering with the co-op." She waited for the applause to end. "I'd like to tell you why we named the co-op Carol's Closet. This past January Lucas Kendrick visited Marietta and—"

"Wasn't he the man who got lost in the snowstorm?" The woman's comment received a round of laughter.

Ava smiled. "There was a reason Lucas came to Marietta. Thirty years ago his nineteen-year-old mother arrived here alone and pregnant with him." The room stilled. "Mable Bramble—" Ava pointed out the older woman "—took

Carol into her home and kept her safe until she delivered Lucas at the hospital. Then Mable helped this young mother and her newborn son get an apartment over on First Avenue.

"Virginia Pritchard, who owned the Main Street Diner back then, hired the young mother as a waitress and allowed her to bring Lucas to the diner while she worked because she couldn't afford childcare."

"Carol left Marietta after two years and sadly she passed away not long ago. Lucas came back to carry out his mother's wishes and thank those who helped them."

Ava's throat grew tight when she caught Mable Bramble wiping a tear away. "I believe if Carol were here today she'd help lead the charge for single mothers to further their education in hopes of providing a better future for their children."

Applause echoed through the store.

"I know Carol's Closet is going to be a huge success because the members of our community are one big family and when one person succeeds we all succeed. Thank you for coming today and now—" Ava smiled at Sandra "—it's time to cut that beautiful cake."

"Hold up," a voice called out from the back of the room. Ava's heart stopped beating when her gaze landed on Lucas. Roger and a woman she didn't recognize stood next to him. The crowd parted and Lucas moved closer.

Sophie shrieked when she saw him. "Mr. Lucas!"

He hugged her daughter and Ava's eyes burned with unshed tears.

"Princess Sophie, I've missed you." Lucas smiled at Ava.

"I knew it would work," Sophie said.

"What would work?" he asked.

"If I wore my princess crown, you would come back."

Ava wiped away a tear, hoping she wouldn't bawl in front of everyone.

Lucas glanced around the room. "I hope you'll indulge me for a few minutes while I tell this single mother how much I love her." His blue eyes trapped Ava's gaze and the crowd around them became a blur of color.

Lucas grasped Ava's hands. "You rode into my life on a blast of cold air and captured my attention. I knew the moment I saw you that you were special." He squeezed her fingers. "And it wasn't just because you were beautiful. I could see your heart in your eyes, Ava. You put the needs of others before yourself. In a world full of people only looking out for number one, you're caring for everyone else."

Tears pooled in her eyes and Lucas's image wavered.

"When I'm with you, I see more of what's right in this world than what's wrong. Life is full of uncertainties." He pressed her hand against his chest. "But in my heart, Ava Moore, you're the one sure thing that makes sense."

She sucked in a breath when he knelt on one knee. "I fell in love with you inside that Dumpster." Murmurs broke out and Lucas spoke over his shoulder. "We'll explain later." After the room grew quiet, he said, "Nothing in this world would make me happier than making a life with you and Sophie right here in Marietta. Will you marry me, Ava?"

"Yes, I'll marry you, Lucas." He slid a breathtaking solitaire diamond onto her ring finger then stood and pulled her into his arms. Applause and cheers echoed around them as they kissed.

Lucas looked at Sophie and said, "Wait right here, princess." He walked over to the door and retrieved the picnic basket sitting on the floor. This time he knelt in front of Ava's daughter. "Princess Sophie, would you do me the honor of allowing me to be your father?"

"If you're my daddy does that mean you're gonna come back and sleep on Mommy's couch again?" Laughter erupted around them and Ava felt her cheeks grow warm.

"If I'm your daddy, I'll buy us a house to live in."

"Do I still get to be a princess if you marry Mommy?"

"You'll always be my little princess, no matter how old you grow."

"Do I get a ring, too?" Sophie asked.

"Princesses don't get rings," Lucas said.

Sophie's brown eyes blinked. "What do they get?"

Lucas lifted the lid on the basket. "They get puppies."

Sophie squealed when a fluffy black-and-white fur ball poked its head out of the basket.

Ava's heart burst with happiness and the tears she'd tried to restrain rolled down her cheeks. Sandra shoved a tissue into her hand then wiped her own eyes. Sophie flung her arms around Lucas's neck. "I love you, Daddy."

"I love you, too, Princess Sophie."

The puppy licked Sophie's hand and she giggled. "What's his name?"

"It's a her and you get to choose the name," he said.

"I'm gonna name her Cinderella," Sophie said.

Lucas laughed. "I thought you might." He grabbed Ava's hand and they moved out of the way so Sophie could show everyone her new puppy.

"What about your job and—" Lucas pressed his finger against her lips. "I'll tell you about it later." He kiss to her then said, "Marietta has always been home; it just took a while to find my way back."

A throat cleared and Lucas turned. Roger approached them with a woman Ava didn't recognize. "I'd like you to meet my wife, Claire."

"Pleasure to meet you, Ava." Claire waved a hand in the air. "This dress shop is gorgeous. I may have to buy something before we leave town."

Roger hugged Ava. "I couldn't have picked a finer woman for my son. Take care of my boy." Roger released her then said, "Now where's my granddaughter?"

Sophie appeared with the puppy in her arms. "Look, Mr. Roger, I got a Cinderella puppy." Roger pronounced Cinderella the prettiest dog he'd ever seen then Sophie tugged the hem of Claire's dress. "Are you Mr. Roger's queen?"

Claire smiled at Roger. "Why yes, I am, young lady."

Roger made a goofy face and Sophie giggled.

"There's a pet carrier in the back room for the puppy," Lucas said.

"C'mon, Princess Sophie." Roger took her hand. "Let's show Cinderella her new dog house." Claire followed the pair when they walked off.

"Lucas." Tilly stepped forward and hugged him. "You've made your mother very happy."

"I have?" he said.

Right then a cold burst of air swept past Ava and Lucas. They glanced at the front door, but it remained closed.

"Carol's standing next to you, Lucas," Tilly said. "She wants you to know that she's proud of you for allowing your father to be a part of your life."

Tilly looked at Ava. "And Carol is honored that you named the co-op after her." Ava's mother-in-law glanced to her right and said, "Of course she knows."

"Knows what?" Lucas asked.

"Carol says Ava should know how lucky she is to have her son's love."

Ava stared into Lucas's eyes. "Tell Carol that I promise I will make sure Lucas knows how much he's loved every day for the rest of his life."

Tilly smiled. "She heard."

"When I visited you at your house, Tilly, was my mother there?" Lucas asked.

"Carol showed up the day you stopped to ask me for directions to the hotel."

"That explains why I felt close to my mother when I was around you." His smile faded. "Will my mother be around all the time?"

"Now that you've found Ava, your mother is ready to move on." Tilly grasped Lucas's arm. "Carol says she'll always be watching over you and your family."

"Tell my mother that I love her very much and I miss her every day."

A chilly rush of air blew past them and Tilly smiled. "She

knows."

Lucas cupped Ava's face and stared into her eyes. "We're going to have a beautiful life, together."

Ava decided she owed her daughter an apology. The kingdom of Marietta wasn't out of princes and she'd found herself the very best one... *And they lived happily ever after in the kingdom of Marietta.*

The End

Holiday at the Graff Series

Book 1: Halloween at the Graff by Sincliar Jayne

Book 2: Christmas at the Graff by Kaylie Newell

Book 3: New Years at the Graff by Marin Thomas

Book 4: Valentine's at the Graff by Sinclair Jayne

Book 5: Love at the Graff by Jeannie Watt

Available now at your favorite online retailer!

About the Author

Marin Thomas is an award-winning author of over 35 western romances for Harlequin books and she also writes women's fiction for Berkley/NAL. She loves small-town stories with quirky characters that revolve around the importance of family and is thrilled that her Tule debut will release in the Montana Born line and Chocolate Shop Books series. Marin grew up in Janesville, Wisconsin, and attended college at the University of Arizona where she played basketball for the Lady Wildcats and earned a B.A. in Broadcast Journalism. Following graduation she married her college sweetheart in a five-minute ceremony at the historical Little Chapel of the West in Las Vegas, Nevada. She and her husband live in Phoenix, Arizona, where she spends her free time browsing junk shops for her next story idea and researching ghost tours.

Visit Marin's website www.marinthomas.com.

Thank you for reading

New Year's at the Graff

If you enjoyed this book, you can find more from all our great authors at TulePublishing.com, or from your favorite online retailer.

Made in United States
Troutdale, OR
09/24/2024

23112220R00148